ALIX JAMES

THE
ROGUE'S
WIDOW

A PRIDE AND PREJUDICE VARIATION

Blog and newsletter: https://nicoleclarkston.com/

Facebook: https://www.facebook.com/NicoleClarkstonAuthor

Twitter: (1) Nicole Clarkston (@NicoleClarkston) / Twitter

Amazon: https://www.amazon.com/Nicole-Clarkston

Austen Variations: http://austenvariations.com/

Contents

To Those who bring a smile to my face—this book is for you. I hope I have returned the favor.

One

November 1812

London

Elizabeth Bennet shifted nervously in her chair. The gentleman behind the desk had little enough to say, but the weight of his pensive glances and oddly punctuated sighs was making her hands sweat. He frowned and tapped his quill on the page before him.

She cleared her throat. "Mr Darcy, I can provide another reference if you wish. Perhaps my former neighbours, Sir William and Lady Lucas, who have known me since my infancy?"

He raised a brow. "You need this position badly." It was not a question.

A small part of Elizabeth's heart died. She lowered her eyes and confessed, "I do. There were five of us sisters, and only one other has found work as a governess since my father's death. I—I know I do not have the formal education typically required, and my connections are not—"

"You are perfect," he declared, slapping his pen down on top of her references with finality. "You begin at once." He pushed back his chair and stood, walking around the desk and passing by without a second glance. He stopped near the door, however, and looked back to her. "Are you coming?"

She rose less gracefully than she would have liked, still a bit dazed. "Forgive me, Mr Darcy, but are we not to discuss... ah... details?"

"Do you mean your pay? Naturally." He opened the door and spoke to the footman just outside. "Parker, will you have Mrs Dobbs prepare Miss Bennet's room? And send Martha in with tea."

The footman left, and Mr Darcy walked out into the hall without another word to her. Elizabeth looked hesitantly about, wondering if she ought to follow.

"Miss Bennet, you really must keep up. You will be wishing to send word of your employment to your mother, and you may use the writing desk in the blue drawing room for your purpose while your room is prepared. Have you a change of attire?"

Elizabeth looked helplessly down at her best day gown. "Most of my other clothes have been sold. If these are not suitable, I do know how to make more."

Mr Darcy waved dismissively. "They will do for now, but I had rather wished you had something else to change into, so these would not become soiled."

She blinked. "Soiled?"

"Indeed, for the Marshalsea is not known for cleanliness. Ah, here we are. The writing desk is just there. Pens, notepaper, all in the drawer."

"The Marshalsea! Forgive me, sir, but I thought I was to meet Miss Darcy and discover if I suited her."

"Naturally. My sister is in Derbyshire, and we shall journey there on the morrow."

"Then, I fail to understand..."

He bit back a sigh, as if explaining to a child. "First, your letter. Then tea, then we depart for the Marshalsea. After the ceremonials, I will have a seamstress come measure you for some new garments."

"Sir, for what sort of post have I just been hired?" she demanded. "I answered an advertisement for a lady's companion."

"Indeed."

She spread her hands. "Why am I to accompany you to a debtor's prison?"

"Why, that is where you are to be married, of course."

Elizabeth's knees nearly buckled. "Married!"

"Naturally, for you cannot pass as a suitably respectable companion for a young lady unless you are married or widowed or something of that nature. I certainly cannot have a single gentlewoman living under my roof without—"

"Married!"

He rolled his eyes. "Did no one explain the conditions of the position to you?"

"Only what was in the advertisement. 'A single young lady of gentle upbringing sought as a companion.' That is what the advert said."

"Why, yes, that is what it said. But did no one tell you what it meant? I shall have to speak to Mrs Dobbs about this. Come, Miss Bennet, your letter. We have an appointment to keep."

"Mr Darcy!" Elizabeth's temper flared, and she set down her foot. "I do not mean to put a single drop of ink on paper until I have had a clear explanation of matters. I begin to think this position cannot suit."

He pursed his lips. "Have you a long list of other options?"

Elizabeth hesitated. "I could work as a seamstress."

Mr Darcy snorted. "With fine hands such as yours? You would be turned out within a week for working too slowly. I offer you a perfectly agreeable situation suited to a lady of gentle birth, and a better you will find nowhere."

"In marrying a man I do not know this very afternoon?"

"No one ever said you had to live with him. You needn't even touch him if you do not wish. In fact, I would advise you to discourage any displays of affection—that sore on his lip has become rather ghastly."

"Who is this person to whom you would so blithely wed a complete stranger?"

He stared and crossed his arms. "You really heard nothing of this?"

"No, and I am not certain I wish to."

"But you just asked me. Come, Miss Bennet, you must speak more plainly."

Elizabeth clenched her teeth and closed her eyes, counting to three before she lost her temper with her prospective employer. "What I meant, sir, is that these details you take for granted are vital to my decision about accepting the position. They ought to have been disclosed before, and I am suspicious about why they were not."

"Yes, yes, very well. The man you are to marry was my father's ward. He has a substantial inheritance that will pass to his brother upon his death, which, I daresay, is imminent. For numerous reasons, I prefer that some other will receive his endowment, which is why I took it upon myself to secure for him a bride."

"But I could not inherit! Surely you do not mean for me to bear this man an heir!"

"Did I not explain you needn't touch him? Be easy on that score, for there is no entail to prohibit the widow inheriting. It is a modest estate—Corbett Lodge—worth a little more than one thousand per annum in its present state. It is large enough for five or six ladies and a few servants, I should say, but do not set your hopes on carriages and finery. I am afraid he spent the coffers dry before I had him thrown into debtor's prison, but the land itself should begin to restore—"

"Forgive me, Mr Darcy," she interrupted, "but did you say that you had this man thrown into prison?"

"Who else would have done it?" he asked reasonably. "I assure you, it was a kindness to everyone concerned."

"I do not..." Elizabeth shook her head and started again. "I expect he must have no fond feelings for you."

"Bernard? He despises the very air I breathe. Miss Bennet, do you mean to write your letter to your family or not?"

"I have not decided! Answer me this, sir. Why would this... this Bernard person permit you to choose a bride for him for the sole purpose of diverting his inheritance, if he hates you so much?"

Mr Darcy smiled. "Because the one person in this world Bernard Wickham detests more than myself is his younger brother George."

S HE HAD SPIRIT, THAT much was obvious. And enough dignity to baulk at the notion of wedding a stranger for his inheritance, which spoke well of her character. Moreover, he was quite taken with her looks—that was to say, she would present well in Society, once she had a new wardrobe and a few good meals. Judging by the way her gown fitted about the bodice, it had been some while since she had enjoyed a proper board.

She was silent and grim now, avoiding his gaze across the carriage. She seemed as if she wished to speak with Martha, sitting beside her, but each time she drew a breath, her eyes flicked toward him and then she subsided. Darcy mentally added another virtue to her account: she did not talk overmuch.

What she did say, however, tended to be rather bold and contrary.

"I still do not understand," she spoke abruptly after some silence.

"What do you not understand, Miss Bennet?" he asked with affected weariness.

"Why not simply let the brother inherit?"

"You will meet him at length, I should guess. I will permit you to answer that question yourself."

"But, then—" she gestured in exasperation. "Why me?"

He frowned, cast his eyes up to the roof of the carriage, and then lifted his shoulders. "Why not?"

"You know nothing of me, my character, my experience."

"I thought you a suitable companion for my sister. Be assured that I am more selective of her company than Bernard's."

"But how do you know I will not find some way to take advantage of the situation?"

He chuckled low in his throat. "Pray, when you do find a way, be my guest. I have tried to turn my hand to a better circumstance and failed. The 'inheritance' you are to receive is no gift, madam. The house and property are in complete disrepair. It is sufficient for you to shelter your mother and sisters, and as we discussed, your 'pay' as Georgiana's companion is to be the upkeep on the house until the property can support itself again."

"But it makes no sense—that is outrageously extravagant!" she cried.

"I know it is, but I have my reasons. I can see that you are practiced in the art of economy." At this, she reddened and glanced self-consciously down at her apparel.

He continued. "Your family will have a modest allowance, and I trust you will exhort them not to spend through it too quickly. Three hundred pounds between them ought to be sufficient for their expenses, I should think."

"Three—" She coughed. "Three hundred is more than we have seen in better than two years, and many times what a lady's companion makes."

"I cannot very well expect four women to go about without respectable attire or manage a house without a sturdy maid and a reliable man of all work. My own steward has long overseen Corbett's rents and income, so there is no need to concern yourself with those affairs. And I will cover the necessary repairs to the roof. It ought to have been done when Bernard first inherited the land, but it was not. Ah, here we are, and I see the parson is already arrived. Welcome to the Marshalsea, Miss Bennet. What do you think of the new building?"

She looked dubiously out the window, her complexion picking up a faint hint of yellow. "Are you certain of this, Mr Darcy?"

"You will suit my needs perfectly, Miss Bennet."

The young lady shot him a look that could have scalded ice. "And I have your word as a gentleman that you will treat me with dignity?"

"Miss Bennet! What do you take me for, your future husband? I assure you, we are not cut from the same cloth. Disguise is my abhorrence; my offer is genuine."

She looked only somewhat mollified and heaved a shaken breath. "Then let us get on with it."

B ERNARD WICKHAM DID NOT enjoy the favour of the guards. While some of the prison's inhabitants possessed charm or agreeable visitors, Bernard regularly incurred the disdain of all by his filth, his vulgar ways, or his incessant snivelling. Thus, when they all filed into Bernard's cell, they found the dying man with no attendant to minister to his wants. Only the provisions supplied by Darcy himself lent him comfort, and half of those looked to have been bartered away for drink.

"Darcy," Bernard rasped. "Is that you?"

Miss Elizabeth stirred beside him. "Bernard has lost his sight," he muttered quietly. "The final stages of his disease."

"But not my hearing. Have you brought me a woman?"

"I have brought a lady."

Bernard tried to sit up on his stained mattress. "Is she blonde? You know I will only have the blondes. Does she have wide hips? A man likes a handful—"

Miss Bennet gasped beside him, her hand to her mouth. Darcy turned to her with a placating expression and a soothing gesture, then spoke again to Bernard.

"I daresay you had a few too many handfuls in your day. Miss Bennet is trim with dark hair, and far too good for you in any case."

"Come, Darcy, if I am to marry the wench, she can at least keep me warm."

"That was not our agreement. Are you ready? I will call for the parson."

Bernard coughed into a bloody cloth and then spat on the floor. "Curse you, Darcy. Call him and be quick about it lest I die before it is done."

Darcy opened the door and invited the parson in. The man of God looked doubtfully about the chamber, glancing between bride and groom with raised brows. "A word, please, Mr Darcy."

Darcy walked with the man to the corner. "Is something amiss?"

"Sir, the license is in order and I see that you have even drawn up the proper settlement papers, but this ceremony you ask me to perform is a mockery to the holy institution of—"

"Does not your scripture command us to look after widows and orphans in their distress?"

The parson narrowed his eyes. "It does."

"And that is no less than my friend wishes to do in his last days. Would you begrudge him the chance to carry out one redeeming act at the end of his life?"

"Mr Darcy, a marriage requires consummation to be recognised as complete, in the hopes that there be symbolic union and some issue."

"And how do you know there will be no such thing?" Darcy asked in a low voice that Miss Bennet would not overhear. "It is not for me to interfere in the affairs between a man and his wife."

The parson scowled for a full minute, glancing back and forth between Darcy and Bernard. "Very well." To the couple, he spoke next. "Mr Wickham and Miss Bennet, are you prepared?"

Darcy looked to the lady and saw her countenance was now a nauseated shade of green. She was curling her lip in distaste as Bernard sat up and made some crude reference to her chastity.

"They are both ready," Darcy answered for them. The look in Miss Bennet's eyes spelled murder, but she held her tongue.

"Miss Bennet, will you stand here? And you must take your betrothed's hand. I absolutely insist upon this much." The parson turned a stern look on Darcy as Miss Bennet shrank from Bernard's diseased flesh.

"Here." Darcy produced a handkerchief and wrapped it over her fingers as she stared open-mouthed back at him. "I am a man of my word, Miss Bennet."

She took it with a last scathing glare, and a few moments later, Mrs Bernard Wickham tossed the handkerchief back in his face with a vengeance.

Spirited, indeed.

Two

*W*HAT HAD SHE JUST *done?*

Elizabeth fought down another wild surge of panic as the truth of the last four days shook her breath once more. Was she truly...? She closed her eyes and extended her left hand, then cautiously peeked at that fourth finger. That was still a ring.

Was not the husband supposed to provide such a token himself? Yet, she was somehow bound to such a poor excuse for a spouse that his friend—if that was what Mr Darcy was—had produced the gold band. And the license. And a trousseau, of sorts, if the five new gowns and the trunk full of personal apparel that had appeared in her room were truly hers.

And now, during the time in which many couples took wedding tours, she was in a carriage bound for work in Derbyshire, with a man whose expectations were a mystery and whose very presence was bewildering. She hoped desperately that his sister did not resemble him.

"Halt," Mr Darcy ordered the driver. The carriage stopped, and he dismounted and walked away with no word of explanation. Elizabeth watched him curiously and waited.

"Mrs Wickham, the house will not improve in appearance for your delay," he summoned.

Elizabeth leaned over the maid, a little farther towards the open door and beheld the prospect she had not seen through the window. Slowly she uncurled her stiff legs and made her careful way down from the coach. A gentleman would have stepped back to help her, but Mr Darcy only watched from several feet away as a footman performed the task.

Perhaps it was because she was no longer Elizabeth Bennet of Longbourn, daughter of a man of leisure, whose name and person commanded the respect of any who would call himself a gentleman. No, she was now Mrs Wickham, a woman of reduced circumstances in the employ of others. She had thought herself prepared for all that accompanied her change in status, but it seemed she was not.

Still, her circumstances were not all bleak. Mr Darcy stood with his thumbs tucked into the pockets of his coat, as if impatient for her to catch up. When she did, he pointed disinterestedly at the stone house just below the rise on which they stood. "Corbett Lodge, such as it is."

Elizabeth felt the warmth rising in her breast. A house—a real house, large enough for all her family! This made everything worthwhile.

"The stonemasons come next week, and the roof is to be re-tiled as soon as the rains hold off. I will have the cow shed re-thatched, as well. Bernard promised to pay me back for the expense of all the repairs."

Elizabeth rolled her eyes up to the gentleman. "With what?"

"He said I could take it out of his whiskey allowance." Mr Darcy's voice was perfectly flat, but Elizabeth thought she detected a curve to the left side of his mouth. He had not made a jest, had he?

"I expect the house will be habitable again in just over a month, weather permitting," he continued. "But it may take longer to rid it of the rats."

"Rats!"

"And pigeons. But Bernard says they are fine company, and juicy to eat."

Elizabeth shuddered. "I hope you are in jest again, sir."

He turned with a half smile. "Speaking of victuals, let us go."

G EORGIANA DARCY DID NOT resemble her brother, either in looks or in personality.

The young lady was of better-than-average height and a sturdy, long-limbed build, with fair hair and the lightest blue eyes Elizabeth had ever seen. She felt keenly the contrast to her own less fashionable appearance—darker and more shapely—but Georgiana Darcy was such an unaffected character as to make Elizabeth forget her discomfort nearly as soon as it had been conceived.

Mr Darcy had, much to Elizabeth's surprise, exerted himself to three or four sentences together when he introduced them. After so doing, however, he promptly called for tea in his study and left them.

"Do not trouble about my brother, Mrs Wickham," Miss Darcy apologised. "He is always a trifle weary when he comes home, having seen and spoken to far more people than he wishes. Fear not, he will be his usual personable self by tomorrow."

"Do you mean I have been treated only to half his good humour?" Elizabeth asked. "Perhaps the other half is the one that knows how to smile. I dearly hope he has not mislaid it!"

Miss Darcy giggled. "He found you, did he not? And he must have been in one of his odd humours when he did so. Why, you do not look or sound at all like a proper lady's companion!"

"My goodness! If you mean to begin our acquaintance by doubting my credentials, I shall have to answer you very tartly indeed, Miss Darcy."

The girl laughed in earnest, hiding her wide grin behind her hands. "I think we shall get on famously, Mrs Wickham."

"Please—" Elizabeth winced. "Would it be improper for you to call me Elizabeth?"

"Well, I should think it would be for you to determine what was proper," Miss Darcy said. "But if you prefer it…"

"Very much. I do not quite feel like a 'Mrs Wickham.'"

"Then Elizabeth it is. I am ever so glad, for I like your own name better anyway. Come, I will introduce you to Mrs Reynolds and we will get you settled."

Elizabeth permitted Miss Darcy to take her arm, and they fell into step together. And for the first time in better than two years, she was no longer afraid of the morrow.

DARCY HEARD HER ENTER his study, just as he had requested. Heard the footman step back unobtrusively from the open door, heard her halting steps as she approached, and even her uneven breaths when she stood before his desk. He had known many a man of power who ignored his guests as a means of asserting dominance, but that was not what made him slow to greet Mrs Wickham. With a flourish, he signed the bottom of the document before him, glanced once more over it to ensure all was as it should be, and then pushed it to the front of his desk.

"I imagine you will wish to approve this." He rose from the chair and walked to the window, permitting her to read it without his scrutiny. He crossed his arms and pretended interest in a winter bird nesting in a tree, but all the while he was listening carefully to her—the way she cleared her throat as silently as possible, the faint gasp as she read the particulars, and the light rustling of the document as she adjusted her fingers.

"Sir... this is not what we had agreed," she said at last.

He turned back. "Is something unsatisfactory?"

"Do you not feel you are being unjust? See, here—" She held aloft the page, her finger indicating the place. "I am to govern my associations to suit you?"

"That is not what it says. As the new residents of Corbett Lodge, the responsibility of overseeing its tenants will naturally fall to you and your family. This document declares your understanding of a landlord's usual duties."

She bristled and held the paper closer to him. "I know perfectly well what those duties are, sir. My father was a gentleman, lest you forget. I speak of the passage just below that."

Darcy narrowed his eyes to read the sentence again. "Why, that is nothing more nor less than the expected. My sister is not to be distressed by undesirable company."

She arched a brow—an expression that never failed to make him pause in reluctant admiration whenever she employed it. "Would you please define 'undesirable' for me, sir?"

"Anyone she does not care to receive, or anyone I would deem an unseemly influence for an impressionable girl of sixteen. I should think that you, as a gentlewoman yourself, would not require me to name specific individuals."

"I see." She quirked her mouth to the side as she read the document to herself once more. A line appeared between her brows. "You mean to send your own carriage for my mother when the house is ready?"

"Would they prefer to ride in a post-chaise?"

She drew breath and shook her head. "No, sir. I... that is very kind."

"It is my duty, Mrs Wickham. As you are employed at Pemberley now, not to mention a neighbour whose husband is not at hand to perform the task, I could countenance nothing less."

A shadow crossed her features at the word "husband," but cleared quickly. "Your terms are acceptable, but what is this 'termination' you speak of in the last paragraph?"

"Merely a clause stating that either of us has the right to dissolve the contract if the other fails to uphold the terms."

She read it carefully, and Darcy could not help but notice how fine and dark her lashes were as they shaded her lowered eyes. "I believe this is the sort of contract one agrees upon before engaging for the position, not after. It is rather too late now for either of us to retract—at least for myself."

"In that case, Mrs Wickham, we would both do well to uphold our own ends of the agreement. I pledged myself to honesty and diligence, and I believe you did as well."

She laid the contract on the desk and took up the pen. "I will not fail, Mr Darcy."

F AILURE WAS THE LAST thing she was worried about.

Miss Darcy was as easy a creature as any Elizabeth had ever met. Enchanting and biddable, talented and kind, the only fault Elizabeth could find with her charge was that Georgiana Darcy seemed insecure around people, particularly men. Elizabeth began gently encouraging the young heiress in conversation and in her duties as the mistress of the manor, and saw some little improvement in only a fortnight.

Pemberley itself was also nothing to complain of. The house was everything splendid—grandeur tastefully married to simplicity—and the grounds were far more than her adventurous and poetic heart could have longed for. Even better, Mrs Reynolds seemed to have taken a special liking to Elizabeth. She could not stir from her room but that the housekeeper appeared to know of it and managed to put some kindness in her way. In fact, every person she met at the estate was a comfort and a delight to her world-weary spirits...

And then, there was the master.

Elizabeth's encounters with Mr Darcy began to follow a pattern which was only predictable in the man's very capriciousness. He would arrive in a room as a great storming gale, an overwhelming presence that instantly drew all eyes and ears under his sway. He never seemed in a temper or even mildly put out, but even if everyone in the room did not answer to him already, they would have found themselves doing so simply because he expected it and gave them no alternative.

It was not that he was rude. Not quite. He spared not a second thought for general niceties of conversation or banal observations about the weather or the day's events. It was as if those means of putting others at ease and diverting the conversation to one's liking were beneath his dignity and beyond his patience. Rather, he would leap into one subject after another with all the grace and tact of an axe felling a giant oak. Once satisfied, he often quit the room as abruptly as he had entered it, with no indication of when the remaining parties therein would see him next.

For the first two weeks, Elizabeth had found his manners terribly unnerving. She never could decide what precisely he expected or thought of her, and that was a novel sensation. In all her prior experience, she had prided herself on her perception of persons, but with Mr Darcy, she was constantly on edge. As a tactic to combat this uncomfortable wariness he inspired in her, she developed a regrettable habit of delivering saucy retorts to his blunter statements. Rather than object, he would sally with something doubly vexing, until Elizabeth could not decide whether they were arguing or teasing one another. Either way, it was all fearfully improper behaviour for a lady's companion and her employer.

One afternoon, a few weeks after Elizabeth had come to Pemberley, Miss Darcy retired earlier than usual to dress for dinner. Elizabeth, restless from far less walking than she had been accustomed to, took the opportunity to venture out into the dormant garden for a bit of fresh air. The exercise proved a balm to her rumpled thoughts, and before she quite understood herself, she had walked over an hour round the paths that were manicured even in late winter.

Just as she was feeling chilled and wishing to return to the house, she saw Mr Darcy cross the path ahead of her. He was on a tall bay horse and glanced almost nonchalantly in her direction as he slowed to a trot, then a walk. After a brief hesitation, he dismounted and approached, leading his horse.

"I trust you approve of the walking paths around the lake, Mrs Wickham."

She clasped her hands together and tried to conceal a shiver. "There are few who could not approve, even at this time of year."

"But you have a discerning eye and a critical tongue, therefore your opinion is more worth the having."

She tilted her head to peer at him under her winter bonnet. "You think me critical, sir?"

"Are you not? But it was not an insult, Mrs Wickham. I value the opinions of those who will give me the unvarnished truth, far more than the silver words of those who mean only to tickle the vanity. What do you think, do the trees hang too low over the path? Should the bank be reinforced around the shallow parts?"

"I found nothing wanting. Moreover, I do not know why you would apply to my expertise, for it is minimal. The only thing I could possibly find lacking is that it was altogether too quiet for my taste."

He surveyed her with a raised brow. "You prefer a large company on your constitutionals, Mrs Wickham?"

"You mistake me. I was longing to hear birds singing, and perhaps a squirrel or two rustling in the trees to break the monotony of the wood, but that is a vain fancy for it is the wrong time of year. But since you ask about my social preferences, I should say that one agreeable companion is far superior to a dozen less agreeable persons."

"And what, in your estimation, constitutes an 'agreeable' companion?"

She pursed her lips and looked up to the trees in thought. "A like mind and good conversation."

He walked several paces before answering. "A like mind, I believe we could produce for you, but what do you call good conversation? A skilled and artful painting of the world by the spoken word? An exudate of feeling, poured out and picked apart by many eager voices?"

"No, indeed. Despise my taste if you will, but I delight in wit and absurdity. You speak of paintings and tapestries, but I liken good conversation more to a chess board. And sometimes, to nothing at all."

"Nothing?"

She drew in a deep breath, closing her eyes and relishing the smell of pine in chilled air. "Sometimes, words only interrupt the harmony. Have you never known anyone with whom you could converse without saying a single word?"

He focused his gaze on the ground before them. "One."

Elizabeth watched him in curiosity. His jaw flexed once or twice, and something flickered about his expression, but he seemed to will it away. They were nearing the house and stables now, and she was glad of the prospect of a warm fire as the afternoon waned.

"Have you been to Lambton yet?" he asked suddenly.

She looked up at him. "Lambton? No, but I suggested to Miss Darcy that we might venture there one day."

He nodded grimly. "Be prepared to be treated differently there."

"Differently? How so, Mr Darcy?"

He stopped, glanced up at the stables ahead, then turned to her. "Bernard Wickham was not loved in Derbyshire any more than he was in London. It may take a few encounters for the townsfolk to understand you were not of his stamp." He lifted his hat without another word, mounted his horse, and jogged towards the stables.

Three

DARCY SHED HIS COAT and called for the fire in his study to be built back up. The outing had been brisk and invigorating, though an extended ride in such cold had been ill advised, at best. A dastardly little sentiment had crept into his thoughts, pricking and wriggling and leaving him no peace until he had satisfied it. The notion that Mrs Wickham, unfamiliar with the surroundings as she was, might have suffered some mishap on her walk had robbed him of his usual serenity. Little else could account for her being out so long on such a cold day, and after fretting near the window where he could see the path for half an hour, he had surrendered to his feelings of disquiet.

Now, appeased and feeling a bit foolish, he could be content that the woman was safely indoors once more. And then, he scoffed at himself. Was he now to become a mother hen to every soul who lived at Pemberley? Or just this one, the woman with the flashing eyes and sharp tongue? Impossible, he scolded himself. Elizabeth Wickham met none of the outward qualifications he required and bore some rather large prohibitions. One, in particular, was insurmountable—and it was not the fact that she worked for him.

He sank into his desk chair, breathing in the familiar aroma of the world of responsibility. It was clarifying and drew his mind back to the present so he could address the stack of letters his steward had brought while he was out. The top, bearing the seal of Lady Matlock, brought a smile of both pleasure and wistfulness as he opened it.

My dearest nephew,

Your uncle and I were dreadfully disappoint-
ed to hear you were in London just before the
Christmas season, and we did not know of it

until you had gone. We had counted on having you to Matlock House for Twelfth Night, but the messenger returned with word that you had already gone back to Pemberley. And on such roads! I wonder at you, Fitzwilliam, for coming and going in such haste. That is the way Lord W—'s carriage was overturned last year, as you recall that sad event.

I had a letter from Georgiana only last week, in which she declared her expectation that you would return with a new companion for her. As I now presume that was the purpose of your journey, I wonder that you did not consult me! By the time you receive this, you will have been returned long enough to know whether the new companion will suit. I beseech you, write at once if you discover that a replacement is needed. I will interview the woman myself, for our dear Georgiana's concerns are close to my heart.

We had all the family to dinner two evenings ago, for Lady Catherine and Anne desired a return to the milder climes in Kent. As the roads had been reported sound, and the weather was warming somewhat, they departed yesterday. Richard remained in London and did not appear to sorrow overmuch at the prospect of solitude, but I was most troubled at his response when your uncle asked after you. Have the two of you quarrelled? I had not thought any rift possible between you, but I wonder if you held ill feelings after he wed Anne. Do put them aside, Darcy, for the matter is done. Though Lady Catherine still mourns how it has all come out, I would hope you might not. I trust you will write to him at once and sort the matter, for it distresses me greatly to see conflict in the family.

Our dearest Sophia is well. You recall, Darcy, that Mortimer's death has left her a substantial fortune, but she has elected to live again with us rather than at her husband's estate. Your uncle and I thought that suitable, for she is still young enough to be mistaken for a debutante, and just as beautiful as when last you saw her. I expect in six months when she puts aside the mourning garb, she will receive a flurry of callers. I hope you will be at your leisure to visit us at Matlock next summer, for I have always been very fond of you.

I have enclosed a letter for Georgiana. There are a few things I wished to begin discussing with both of you regarding her come-out next year. However, I will leave them for later, as your uncle has determined we must attend a dinner this evening and I retire now to dress.

Affectionately,

Lady Matlock

Dear Mama,

E LIZABETH LIFTED HER PEN and gazed at the fire in her room. She ought to write—she wrote every Wednesday, and her mother would fret if she did not receive her regular letter. But what to say that she had not already said?

Miss Darcy sends her regards.

Miss Darcy always sent her regards.

Derbyshire is beautiful.

There were only so many ways to assure her mother that they were not removing to a wasteland in the wild north.

The new roof on Corbett Lodge is underway.

The surest way possible to make her mother inspect it daily for leaks.

Mr Darcy is outrageously handsome, but the most aggravating man alive...

No, that would certainly not do! She nibbled her lip and set her pen back on the page.

How I miss each of you! I am assured that we will see each other again soon. I thank Providence that we will be happily secured as a family once more by spring. I received a letter from Jane at last. She said she was moved to joyful tears and gave her notice at once to her employers, though I fear it may be some months before she can come to us.

Has Kitty recovered from her cough? Mrs Reynolds gave me a receipt for an elixir that might soothe her, and I will enclose it. I hope Mary enjoyed the book I sent last week. It was one that Miss Darcy purchased for her brother at Christmas, but after she left the room, he asked me if any of you would like it. Mr Darcy said he would have discarded it, as he has three copies already, but he does not subscribe to the destruction of books. It was altogether an odd conversation, as most conversations with him are, but I believe he was meaning to be generous.

I am concerned about what you say of Lydia, that she was flirting with the officers. Mama, I implore you, do keep a close watch on her. We need no longer be distressed for our futures, for you all have a home here in Derbyshire soon. It is not as if we will starve now if we do not catch husbands, and I fear for appearances if my sister is found in some indiscretion. It would be better if she were to go to our uncle Gardiner again until you all come here, but if not, pray do not let her go out without a proper chaperon.

I trust you passed Twelfth Night in comfort and good cheer? You probably suspected that we were engaged with balls and revelry at such an estate as I have told you Pemberley is, but we were a quiet house. Mrs Reynolds did mention the extravagance of the parties given by the late Mrs Darcy, but after her death the family have kept rather to themselves over the holiday.

You have asked me each week to give you my impression of Mr and Miss Darcy, and each week I have demurred until I knew them better. It is a month now, so I shall do my best to comply. Miss Darcy is a sweet girl of barely sixteen. She is nearly unequalled on the pianoforte and paints exquisitely. She speaks four languages and is gracious to all, including myself. She dislikes large groups of people and is entirely petrified of dancing, a skill I have been helping her to improve upon. I do believe her to be the bashful sort, easily troubled by the worry of giving offence even if none was intended. For that reason, I believe some might mistake her for a haughty character, unless they troubled themselves to know her better.

Mr Darcy is more difficult to sketch. Papa would have liked him immensely, for Mr Darcy would have proved a stimulating companion for all of five minutes. Once their conversation had done, I expect they both would have returned to their books and said not another word for two hours together. I can find no fault in his character and his servants all speak well of him, but I am constantly perplexed by trying to discover the answers to questions such as what and why and where... I suppose I must content myself with the understanding that I am no longer the daughter of the house and privy to all the master's concerns.

It is a most trying resolution, for never have I encountered an individual who inspired more curiosity—and occasionally annoyance—in his disposition and motives, but I am determined, and therefore I will succeed in ignoring both Mr Darcy's peculiarities and my own inquisitiveness. If you think of me in your prayers each evening, pray that I do not behave discourteously in my efforts.

I remain yours most affectionately and in hopes of embracing you soon,

Elizabeth

I T WAS INSUPPORTABLE—UNTHINKABLE.

Darcy stared devotedly at the pages of his book, blotting out the other occupants of the room. The ladies would not mind if he said nothing—they ought to be accustomed to his silences by now. Georgiana knew him well enough, and his growing familiarity with the new Mrs Wickham had taught him one other thing about her—a thing he was not altogether pleased to have discovered. She could brood as thoroughly and laboriously as he.

What had passed through her mind on that first journey from London, as she gazed out one carriage window and he out the other? What did she consider when she wandered out into the cold outdoors, or stared into the fire by evening? Certainly, he knew no other ladies who could fall into deep, ponderous thought for hours on end, without troubling him for mundane chatter to soothe their nerves.

Darcy raised the book he was trying to read a little higher, hoping with it he might block his own view of the ladies at the pianoforte. His vision might be obstructed, but his ears were not. And they rang pleasantly with the sounds of feminine laughter and musical harmony.

Mrs Wickham—drat, but that name suited her ill—was no great talent. Rather, she was clearly unschooled in classical forms and her voice, while charming, carried no remarkable quality of melody. Still, hers was a voice he could listen to without desiring to be elsewhere, a thing that could be said for only a handful of persons. But it was dashedly irksome that she had to be so enchanting while he was in the same room.

Georgiana liked her. That was a wondrous comfort, for his sister had been ill at ease since her near disastrous attachment three months previous. And that was why he had settled on Elizabeth Bennet—she possessed just enough cheek to shake Georgiana from her protective shell, but enough practical wisdom to know what it was to plan for the future... to fear for her family's welfare... to take little for herself so that others might have more.

To be sure, his stomach had twisted the first time he had sat at table with her and beheld the faint widening of her eyes at the generous spread, and the meagre portions she chose thereof. With each passing day, she had seemed to settle a little more, but there was still a hint of discomfort when Georgiana would press her to try one more buttered biscuit, one more sweet roll. But those same eyes had taken on a healthy sparkle in these last weeks that was altogether new.

Darcy shook his head and tried to read another line of his book.

"William? William, did you hear that?"

"What?" He dropped the book at last. Georgiana was flitting toward him in that girlish way she still had, her toes light on the carpet as she came to clasp his hand and coax him to his feet.

"Elizabeth said she would play for us and you can teach me how to dance the Allemande. Come, do not be a rock on the sofa all night."

He stood reluctantly, and Mrs Wickham applied herself to a lively, if not flawless tune. Georgiana was no more skilled than the musician—all legs and arms, she was. The graceful girl she was had vanished when the music began. She was probably thinking of the last time she had danced with a man—not himself. It was a memory that ought to make her as uncomfortable as it made him.

"No, Georgiana, like this," he tried to explain. Yet, she kept twisting to the side whenever he would try to step dos-à-dos with her. "No, you must fall back. Has not your dance master taught you this?"

Georgiana pushed away, her expression taut and frustrated, as the pianoforte went quiet. "Oh, I shall never get this! Yes, my master tried to teach me, but I have never yet managed it. Elizabeth said I should try with you, but I cannot picture how it goes. If I could see it done—oh! Elizabeth, you must come show me."

Mrs Wickham's hands dropped from the piano. "I am sure that is unnecessary, Miss Darcy."

"No, it is! Come, William is a fine dancer. You mustn't let this last performance with me make you think otherwise."

Reluctantly, Darcy bowed to Mrs Wickham when she drew near. She curtsied gravely as Georgiana began to play, then her chin came up in near defiance with those first few steps. "If it is any comfort to you, sir, I despise dancing."

"Indeed? How should that be a comfort to me?"

"I would not wish you to suppose that I could accidentally enjoy your discomfiture." They turned twice, she gracefully spiralling about on her toes and ending perfectly positioned beside him.

"I am not discomfited, Mrs Wickham. Are you?"

"Not in the least, sir." She casually tipped her forearm to the side for him to take her hand, her eyes locked straight forward.

"And I suppose you do not care for balls?" he asked.

"Perhaps I have never been to one."

He clasped her hand and felt her back sliding against the inner part of his arm. She was warmer than he had expected. And softer. Remarkable what several weeks of Pemberley's best had done for her figure.

"I believe you are misleading me, Mrs Wickham," he said after a moment of silence. "You seem far too familiar with the steps for one who has never been to a ball."

"It is not misleading to suggest an alternative supposition. I only said 'perhaps.' I did not declare it as a fact."

"In that case, 'perhaps' I dislike dancing as much as you do," he replied.

"Is it the dancing or the environment in general you dislike? Or perhaps it is the music or the selection of partners that displeases you?" She tipped her chin round to him for the first time, and he glanced down into her eyes... and immediately wished he had not done so.

"'Perhaps' it is none of these," he answered. "And 'perhaps' I am being as oblique as you, speaking in false trails and riddles."

"What is a false trail, but an option not explored? And what is a riddle, but a kernel of truth taken out of context?" A faint curve appeared at the corner of her mouth, though she still did not look at him. Her shoulder pressed against his until he crossed his hands and invited her to pirouette under his arm. The way she floated by his side, each step sweetly musical—this was a woman who knew the ballroom floor; knew it well, was mistress of the evening when she stepped out. Her eyes met his, and a hint of amusement played at their corners. "Any sensible employer would consider me impertinent for such speech."

"Madam, impertinent does not begin to describe you. Any sensible lady's companion would think better of her manner."

She laughed, and her eyes... egad, they danced. Darcy caught his breath in some astonishment at the queer sensations panging against his ribs.

"If you wish to reprimand my manner, you may. It is your house, after all. But I am afraid you have made it nearly impossible to dismiss me." She tipped her head with a rather provocative expression, then made a graceful parting gesture with her left hand, taking care to flash that gold ring as she did so.

He stepped back, permitting her to rejoin his sister at the pianoforte. Odd, how she could be so... so present and sharp when she spoke to him, and yet seconds later, her attention was wholly fixed on Georgiana.

As it should be, he reminded himself. At last, he had secured for Georgiana a companion who truly seemed to take an interest in her. A lady of poise and elegance, and yet raw, simple humanity lay close upon the surface. There was a gentleness in her, for all her tart speech and irreverence. And she was clever... far too clever.

Hopefully, he would not regret that.

Four

E LIZABETH'S MOTHER CLUTCHED HER hand as their coach drew to the front of the house. "Lizzy, is it true? We are to live in a real house again? Oh, my dearest girl, pinch me if it is not true!"

Elizabeth grimaced, for the pinching was being inflicted upon her own hand. "It is true, Mama. Corbett is to be your home now. No more living as the poor relation, no more saving all month for bread or dividing us between our relatives or thinking of going out as a governess." As if her mother could have passed for a governess.

Mrs Bennet's eyes were moist, and she looked as if she might expire with her next breath. "My clever Lizzy! How it used to annoy me when your father called you the clever one, but it is true! How daring and wonderful of you to marry so prudently! Always thinking of your poor mother, you are."

"It was not entirely my idea, Mama," Elizabeth protested, but her mother was beyond hearing. She was tumbling down from Mr Darcy's coach, which had brought Mrs Bennet and her remaining daughters from their most recent abode with Mr and Mrs Philips. Elizabeth waited for Lydia, Kitty and Mary to disembark in all their rowdy commotion before attempting the step herself.

"Oh, Lizzy!" Kitty cried. "You did not say the chicken coop was already full! We shall have fresh eggs every day. And look, Mama! There is a cow!"

Mrs Bennet was clutching Mary's arm now, dabbing her eyes and sobbing incoherently. "If only Jane were here," she blubbered, "we would have everything. Why would she not come when we wrote?"

"Mama," Elizabeth soothed, "Jane is a woman of her word, and she gave it to the Robertson family. They are searching for a replacement for her, and she will come when she can."

"But how silly!" insisted Mrs Bennet. "She is a lady of leisure! How dare they keep her?"

Elizabeth gave up and merely took her mother's other arm to guide her into the stone house that now belonged to them. It was nearly the size of Longbourn but was not nearly so well kept. Mr Darcy had a horde of men working on it for weeks, and Elizabeth had spent every waking minute there that had not been devoted to Miss Darcy. The house was now rid of the stench of old filth, but the chimney piece was still crumbling, the kitchen yet showed evidence of a recent fire, and many of the floorboards in the upper rooms were liable to splinter into unsuspecting bare feet. But the roof was patched, and it was all hers.

In a manner of speaking.

She had not been without her moments of panic, self-loathing, and worry. Mr Darcy's ludicrous plan had been carried off before she had quite known what to think, but now she had had time to reflect. Indeed, she had provided her mother with a home in which to pass her later years, and a place for her younger siblings to grow to maturity away from the questionable influence of officers.

But she had traded her father's good name for that of a reprobate, and all for financial gain. That deed still dragged at her heart in her weary moments, causing her inner parts to bubble and twist in moral torment. And each time she would suffer, she could not help but think with a mixture of vexation and gratitude on the man responsible for her present state. It was all the fault of—

"Mr Darcy is so terribly kind to us!" exulted Mrs Bennet. "Why, the larder is full! And is that a smoked ham? Oh, Lizzy, we've not had one of those since... well, never mind."

"Lizzy, what is Miss Darcy like?" Kitty wondered. "Did you not say that Pemberley manor is but three miles away? Why, we shall be the very jolliest of friends!"

"I would not pin your hopes on that, Kitty," Elizabeth said diplomatically. "Miss Darcy is... well, she is a very sweet girl, but I do not think her brother would permit—"

"But she is my own age, is she not?" Kitty whined. "Why should we not be close friends? What other young ladies are in the neighbourhood but her?"

"Yes, Kitty, but you forget that Miss Darcy is of a different sphere," Elizabeth explained. "It is not the same for her."

"Oh, bother with Miss Darcy anyway," Lydia interrupted. "I want to hear about Mr Darcy. Is it true he owns half of Derbyshire?"

"No, Lydia."

"But he is vastly wealthy, is he not? Why, that carriage we rode in is probably his oldest and smallest one. And I heard he is fearfully handsome and had his heart broken by a woman!"

"Who said that?" Elizabeth asked.

"Oh, why, simply everyone I asked at the last coaching inn. Well, I suppose it was only one or two. Or was it just the kitchen maid? Anyway, she said he was betrothed once, and the lady left him for his best friend. Or was it a cousin? Anyway, it was all a great secret."

"How mysterious!" Kitty squealed. "There is nothing quite so alluring as a man who needs his heart mended."

"I am sure I am not interes—"

"Dear heavens!" Kitty whimpered as she swayed in place. "Is that him?"

Elizabeth turned and saw the tall caped rider approaching at a brisk canter. "It is," she sighed.

M R DARCY'S FACE YIELDED no expression as he came near. Not that she expected much, for the man was harder to read than Herodotus. By the time he drew rein, Kitty and Lydia were gripping each other's hands in giggling anticipation and eyeing him like he was a prize ram at the market.

Fortunately, Mary had seen their mother inside. Elizabeth tried to shush the others and send them in as well, but they had no intention of leaving. She turned and offered a curtsy.

"Mr Darcy?"

He nodded and swung to the ground. "Mrs Wickham." He left the rein draped about the horse's neck and began to walk towards the trees.

After two months of acquaintance, Elizabeth no longer lingered behind in confusion when he behaved thus. She did glance back to see whether his horse would wander away, but it never did. She jogged to keep up and see what he had to say.

"I bring papers from London. You may be interested to know that as of twenty-eight January, eighteen hundred and thirteen, you are officially the widow of the former Bernard Andrew Wickham, and all his property and effects are now legally your own."

She stopped. "I am... sorry, I suppose."

Mr Darcy turned to face her. "My condolences in your time of grief, madam."

She shot him a sour look. "You know perfectly well I do not mourn a man I never knew."

"But you must keep up the appearance. While at Pemberley, I am afraid I must insist on full mourning attire, for he was well known to everyone there. Unfortunately. When you are here in your own house, you may go about as you wish, but you must absolutely wait a full year before remarrying."

"What of his debts? Surely, I must now satisfy those."

"What do you have to settle them with?" Mr Darcy arched a brow. "You may spare your breath, for I had bought all of Bernard's debts when I had him committed to prison. As I held them, there is nothing left to repay."

"But I am now the beneficiary of his estate, not you. How does it not follow that I must pay them back?"

"Because," he growled in near exasperation, "I cannot accept repayment. That is all you need know."

Elizabeth crossed her arms. "You hated him."

"So I did. So did most people. You would have as well."

"But why are you doing all this?" She spread her arms. "Why bring me on? Why fill the larder and tile the roof and pack my mother in your fancy carriage to come all this way?"

He frowned. "Because I agreed to. It was not for Bernard, I can tell you."

"Then it was the younger brother you wished to thwart?"

Mr Darcy sighed. "Mrs Wickham, I urge you to rethink your accusation. You have been here a few weeks. Others have depended on this estate for generations."

Elizabeth subsided. He was right, after all, and rather than rising to the bait as she was always tempted to do in his company, she ought simply to be grateful. "I presume there is some formality I must undergo?"

"The will and testament are to be read in three weeks in London. We shall go, and Georgiana will remain here. We shall bring your maid for propriety's sake—I am afraid it would not be fitting to bring your..."

Mr Darcy ceased speaking and merely gazed in astonished silence over her shoulder. Elizabeth turned, her stomach dropping in dread of what she might find.

"Lizzy! There is a tree swing!" Lydia's voice was almost lost amid her squeals of terrified delight as Kitty pushed her ever higher. Lydia was kicking out her heels and giving Mr

Darcy a most undignified view of her petticoats, all while waving and shrieking like a hoyden.

Mr Darcy squinted, and his jaw set. "Perhaps I ought to have interviewed a few more of your references, Mrs Wickham."

She tilted a beatific smile back up at him. "It is too late now, Mr Darcy."

He nodded, his eyes drifting disapprovingly back to Lydia before he answered. "So it is."

"NO, GEORGIANA, I AM afraid it would not be suitable to invite Mrs Wickham's sisters to tea." Darcy was speaking through a tight jaw and trying to keep his voice easy at the same time. It was not working.

"Oh, William, I wish you would not call her that. You know how I detest that name," Georgiana said with a pout.

"I expect she likes it no more than you or I do, but it is her name. What shall I call her instead?"

"Well, I call her Elizabeth when we are together, and she seems to prefer it."

Darcy scoffed. "It is hardly dignified or respectful for you to be addressing an older widowed woman by her Christian name."

"What! Older widow? She is only four years older than I, and two months ago she had never even met Bernard. There, do you see? We both always called him by his Christian name."

Darcy spared his sister a sideways smirk. "Because he preferred it himself."

"Well," she sniffed, tossing her head in a manner peculiarly reminiscent of her new companion, "I shall not listen to you regarding Elizabeth."

"But you will listen where her sisters are concerned. The middle one might not be a disgrace, and there is still the eldest whom I have not met. She may be worth knowing, from what I hear, but inviting one of them to tea becomes an open invitation for all. The two youngest sisters are in every way disreputable and offensive."

"Why?" Georgiana tipped her head and stared blankly at him in her most challenging manner. "Did one of them try to kiss you? Shout profanities at passing children? Spend the evening at the inn playing cards?"

"They simply do not comport themselves as they ought. That is the end of it." Darcy turned away as if to quit the room until his sister's voice stopped him.

"But Elizabeth does."

His feet stilled. "Does what?"

"Comport herself as a lady. Why, she is everything polite and gracious."

Darcy narrowed his eyes at the opposite wall, considering her words. "No. She does not comport herself as a 'lady.' Her manner is... something else altogether."

"What do you mean? You cannot think her improper."

He turned slowly back. "Far from it. But she is no lady. She is... something more than that."

Five

"I T ALL STILL SEEMS surreal," Mrs Wickham murmured—more to herself than to him, he suspected. She stared through the carriage window as they rolled away from the solicitor's offices, and then she sat back with a dazed expression.

"Perhaps it is a touch novel," he confessed, "but I daresay you will accustom yourself to the sensation soon enough."

Her lips parted as she surveyed him. "How so? I never even knew what it was to be a wife, and now I am to learn what it is to be a widow—and a widow with a healthy endowment, besides. It feels unjust, for I have done nothing to deserve this man's entire inheritance."

"Trust me when I say that you would not have wished to learn what it would have been to live as Bernard's wife," he retorted with a jerk of his waistcoat.

She fell silent, her dark, brooding eyes fixed on the window. Better the window than himself. There was always something frightful about locking eyes with her. His stomach would flutter, his pulse would jump, and his tongue routinely grew barbs it did not normally possess. What was it about her that set him so ill at ease?

It could be that spark in her countenance. Most women—nay, most people in general—had the light and living crushed out of them by the time they had reached their majority. A weary callous grew over their true selves—a certain hardness of feeling and expression that spoke of worldly thoughts and cares. Mrs Wickham's look was still fresh and honest as a girl, but tempered with... what was that about the edges of her eyes? The soft corners of her voice? Sadness, perhaps, and not a little hard-won wisdom.

"Mr Darcy, is there something wrong with my bonnet?"

He drew a quick breath, snapping from his musings. "Wrong?"

"You were staring in the oddest manner. Should I have worn something more modest? I am afraid I do not know what is suitable for my station as the widow of Mr Wickham."

"You are perfectly suitable." He purposely turned his gaze somewhere else.

"You are certain? You looked rather curious just now."

He shook his head, wishing she would dismiss the matter.

"Was he a gentleman?"

"What?"

She looked down and straightened her skirts. "A gentleman. I could not be certain. Miss Darcy told me that Mr—that 'Bernard' was the son of your father's steward, but that the elder Mr Darcy had taken great pains to secure a gentleman's inheritance and education for him."

"Do you particularly object to being the wealthy widow of a steward's son?"

She blushed and turned her gaze away. "I am hardly wealthy."

"You have an unencumbered estate to your name, and that is a handsome dowry, even if it is small." He nodded towards the window as the carriage drew up before a familiar townhouse. "And to that end, there is someone I desire for you to meet."

She looked sharply up and glanced outside. "Where are we?"

He did not answer but waited for the footman to place the block and then assisted her down. "We are already expected. Ah, there he is."

Charles Bingley stood in the hall to greet them. "Darcy! About time, old friend. I missed you entirely when last you were in London."

Mrs Wickham was tilting her head and scrutinising him curiously. Darcy gave each a tight smile. "Bingley, may I present Mrs Elizabeth Wickham. Mrs Wickham, this is my good friend Charles Bingley."

"Delighted, madam," Bingley greeted her.

Mrs Wickham's brow creased, and then her eyes widened, and she turned an accusing glare... at Darcy.

"CHARMING GIRL, DARCY. WHAT do you know of her?"

Bingley sipped lightly at the brandy, probably trying to give the impression that he was imbibing more than he truly was. Darcy was less circumspect. After four days of travel and another day of business in the same coach as Elizabeth Wickham, he needed a drink.

"Very little. Her father died two years ago, and the heir to the family estate assumed possession at once. Oddly, he had been Lady Catherine's rector for some months before he inherited. I cannot confirm, but there were hints that he offered marriage to one or more of the daughters—possibly even our Mrs Wickham—but was soundly rejected."

"Surely you know more of her by now. She has been Georgiana's companion since November. Does she play or sing?"

Darcy frowned. "Yes, but I try to absent myself from those performances."

"Whatever for? Is she that dreadful on the ear?"

Darcy swallowed another drink. "Quite the opposite."

"Well, what of her family? You said she has four sisters and her mother with her?"

"One sister has not yet come. There is also an uncle in Meryton and another in London. I gather both had sheltered the family to the extent of their abilities. Tradesmen, both—she does not boast an unbroken pedigree."

Bingley chuckled. "And what of my own lineage? You know that would not trouble a man of my station. But I am dreadfully curious about her marriage. Even with the house, how the devil did you persuade her to take that old reprobate?"

"I gave her no other choice. She still has not forgiven me entirely, but I hoped to do better by her this time."

"This time? Oh, Darcy, you do not mean to force her to marry me, do you?"

"What—force? Many are they who would swoon at your feet simply to gain your notice. Mrs Wickham will count herself fortunate."

"And certainly, I would count myself a fortunate man if we learned to like each other well enough, and you know I would always take your advice. If you told me I ought to marry her, I would do my best to win her affections, but the lady must agree."

"It would suit both of you. She is like to have a dozen rascals sniffing about her skirts before her year of mourning is up. I would see you first in line."

Bingley laughed and gestured with his glass. "You ought to ask her about that. The last time I saw a woman glare at a man the way she stared you down was when Lady Catherine found out about—"

"Yes, yes," Darcy interrupted testily. "She may not see the merits of the arrangement yet, but we have a year."

"Hmm. A great deal can happen in a year."

Darcy set his empty glass aside. "A great deal has happened in just two months."

April, 1813

N OT ALL FACETS OF her new position were disagreeable. Very few, in fact. Rather, everything but her employer himself suited her perfectly. Even Mr Darcy was a good enough man, but she had never met anyone quite so provoking. Most encounters ended in some clash of wit and will, and she never could quite determine whether he found it sportive or merely irritating. For that matter, she could not decide which it was for herself.

One of the most charming qualities of her position was that each Sunday, Elizabeth was permitted the entire day with her mother and sisters. For one day out of seven, she would put aside the disingenuous mourning garb and return to a semblance of her old self: Elizabeth Bennet of Longbourn. On such days, the book room often called to her, and she would retreat there for hours at a time with something she had borrowed from Pemberley's library.

On this day, however, the stirrings of spring tingled in her limbs, and she determined to make what she could of the neglected rose hedge bordering the front of the house. With a sharp pruning knife in hand and wearing her oldest dress, she appointed the whole of the afternoon for her task. She had been happily working nigh an hour when a masculine voice interrupted her.

"I beg your pardon," said a very agreeable-looking young man. "Would you by any chance know if the mistress is about?"

"Of course, I know," Elizabeth returned. She watched him cautiously and clipped another thorny stem.

He smiled—a winsome expression if she had ever seen one. "Perhaps I beg the wrong question. If your mistress is about, would you ask her if she can spare a moment for her brother-in-law?"

"I am afraid I cannot ask such a question, lest I be accused of madness."

"Madness?" he asked innocently.

"Indeed, for when one talks to oneself, it makes others uneasy."

"Ah!" He doffed his hat. "Then I do have the pleasure of addressing my sister-in-law? I must beg your forgiveness. My name is George Wickham, and I presume you must be…?"

"Elizabeth Wickham. Charmed."

"The honour is entirely mine, madam. I was very sorry to hear of poor Bernard's death. I was in Brighton, you see, and word was slow to reach me. I thought to look in on matters and fancy my surprise when I learned that my good brother had left for me a sister. I trust you are bearing up well in your grief?"

"Well enough, thank you," she answered. "May we offer you something after your travels, sir?"

"No! Goodness, no, thank you. I would not wish to intrude on a widow's home. Ah, but the old house does look fine. I see a deal has been done since last I was here. You are to be commended, madam, for effecting such a change."

Elizabeth glanced over her shoulder. "Mr Darcy's men did most of the repairs."

Mr Wickham looked grave when she turned back to him. "I see. Of course, it would only be his duty." He offered a forced-looking smile. "Always duty with Darcy. I am sure he was doing his duty by my poor brother as well."

"I cannot speak for that," she confessed.

"Of course, you cannot. You would have only heard what Darcy wished—but no! I swore to myself that I would not speak ill of the man. It is a time for mending the past, is it not? And just when I thought I had no family left, I am pleased to find I was mistaken. I hope you will think of me as a friend, Mrs Wickham—indeed, it does sound odd for me to call you thus."

Elizabeth looked into the hedge and cut another stem. "As you are my brother, you may call me Elizabeth."

"How very kind! And you may call me George if you wish. I am staying at the inn at Lambton, and I hope I will see you often while I remain in town. I had other business in the area," he added in answer to the question in her eyes. "I expect to be some days at least."

"I hope it is nothing serious," she replied neutrally.

"Well, now that depends on the other party. As you are acquainted with him, I expect you know just how obtuse and trying he can be. There I am again! Forgive me, Elizabeth, I shall not speak slander when I came to make a friend. Have you met many of the neighbours?"

She shook her head. "No, for I am most often with Miss Darcy, and she does not generally receive guests."

"Ah, dear Georgiana! I would ask you to give her my greetings, but she might find that awkward if her brother were to learn of it. Well, I should say, take care to make the acquaintance of Mrs Brown, just a mile to the east. She is but a farmer's widow, but she makes the finest rum cake you will ever taste. Where she gets her rum, I shall not ask! And if you can, be certain to meet with Mrs Godfrey over in East Orchards. You will not find a more generous soul."

"I thank you, sir." Elizabeth dipped her head graciously.

"Well, then, I shall be off. I hope we shall meet again." He replaced his hat and mounted a horse that stood nearby.

Elizabeth watched in fascination as he jogged away, reflecting that he seemed not at all the scoundrel Mr Darcy had painted. But then, Fitzwilliam Darcy seemed only to understand people well when they could serve his purpose, and perhaps George Wickham was one who had never bowed to the local royal son.

Six

"CONGRATULATIONS, DARCY, YOU SUCCEEDED at last."

Darcy scarcely looked up when George Wickham was announced at his study. He had been expecting this, and had even given the order that the rascal was to be admitted when he called at last. The only wonder was that it had taken nearly three months to come about. He never even set aside his quill as Wickham dropped into the chair opposite his desk without being invited.

"I have succeeded at many things," Darcy answered mildly. "Pray, to which are you referring?"

Wickham put his hands on the desk. "Bernard married on his deathbed? Tell me that was not your doing."

"Why would I tell you that? It most certainly was." Darcy dipped his quill and continued writing.

"For what purpose? Oh, I remember!" Wickham leaped from the chair and paced the study, punctuating his words by smacking one fist on the opposite palm. "You swore I would never inherit. You vowed to see me in penury. You promised your revenge for—for what, I do not know."

"Do you not? You do not recall your many offences against my family?"

"I recall that your father loved me, and so did Georgiana. I recall how that made you insensible with jealousy and that you did all in your power to discredit me!"

"No, I did all in my power to protect others from your lies. Where would Georgiana be if I had not intervened? Why, abandoned and probably pregnant out of wedlock, living off the charity of strangers wherever you left her."

"There you are wrong, Darcy! Had you not intervened, she would be comfortably installed as my wife at a charming house three miles from here."

"Just as your previous conquest, I trust?"

"Now, that is unfair. The lady toyed with my affections, not the reverse. Ask her yourself—or have you? Is that why I have not seen Fitzwilliam of late? I ought to call on him and ask after his wife," he mused with a smirk.

"It will not work, Wickham. I've no interest in dredging up the past, and no intention of giving another farthing to a man who gambled away his inheritance within a month of receiving it."

Wickham sneered. "You could not live long on five hundred pounds, either."

"You were promised a living. What came of that? You refused to take orders, that is what."

"I was indisposed when you gave the living to another man!"

Darcy snorted. "Indisposed for six months? You were detained by drink and women. You had never undertaken the proper studies and never intended to. I count it a mercy that you are no man of the cloth."

Wickham returned to the chair and leaned forward intently. "Say what you will, Darcy. I ought to have at least been given Bernard's inheritance. We both knew he had the French disease for years—it was only a matter of time. Yet you hastened his death by having him thrown into debtor's prison and found some desperate wench to marry him at the last moment!"

"Hasten his death, indeed. Bernard was better looked after in prison than he could have been rubbing along in the seedy establishments he frequented. I saw to that. Moreover, I preserved countless innocent maids from his attentions—and from yours!—though it is a shame I was too late for some. That kitchen girl at Corbett, for example—dead at only sixteen because of Bernard. There were others, too, and none of them have a pleasant tale to tell. But I am sure the sentiments of the women you two have ruined do not concern you."

Wickham laughed. "There, you have as much as told me the marriage you brought about was unconsummated."

"I did not ask the lady the particulars of her marital relations, and in the eyes of the Church, the union was satisfactory. Let me also remind you that you will gain nothing by attempting to win her for yourself, for as your brother's widow, the marriage would not be legal."

Wickham sat back in the chair and shook his head. "Neat and tidy. You have thought of everything, Darcy, except for one."

Darcy raised a patient brow. "If you fancy that I spend my days dreaming up means of thwarting you, you have been sadly misled. I have better things to do with my time."

"Aha!" Wickham cried. "I see it. You are dying to know where the flaw is in your arrangements, but you will not ask. Very well, I shall not tell you. But you would be wise to keep an eye on that lovely young widow in the neighbourhood. It would not do for—well! Perhaps I shall say no more. Give Georgiana my regards, will you?"

Wickham breezed out of the room without an adieu, leaving Darcy scowling at his desk. The blackguard, he seethed. Whatever scheme Wickham thought himself the master of, Darcy had no notion. But he would take the man's caution—the last thing he needed was for Wickham to whisper his malcontented perfidy into her ears. She thought little enough of him already.

Not that he would have it differently. It would be too dangerous, should she accidentally take a liking to him. No! That, he could not withstand. Best to keep her at arm's length as his employee—

As the kindest friend Georgiana had ever had. As a local widow, for whom he was occasionally pleased to do a good turn. And as a pleasant neighbour who was already doing much to improve circumstances for the tenants of the neglected estate.

As a beautiful woman... one who needed him just enough to draw him in, but was independent enough to push him away.

Dear heaven, it was too late for him, and he was only just confessing it to himself.

He noted the time on his mantel clock and rose from his desk to go to the window. Precisely four of a Sunday afternoon... and like every Sunday afternoon previous, there was Mrs Wickham, walking up from the garden. As was typical, she had eschewed the offer of a carriage and traversed the three miles from Corbett Lodge on foot. He knew her bonnet-shaded cheeks would be rosy, and her eyes would be bright from the exercise, and she clutched the dour black cape around her shoulders as if she was still not used to it.

She met him as he came out of his study, her head coming up in surprise. Did she know how he waited for her each Sunday afternoon? Or was she truly as oblivious to his notice as she seemed to be?

"Mr Darcy." She curtsied and began to move away.

"I hope your family were well."

She turned and dipped her head slowly. "They were. I trust Miss Darcy is changing for dinner?"

"I presume. I understand you had a visitor today at Corbett."

She began to pluck the gloves from her fingers without looking at him. "I have many visitors. The estate has eight tenants, you know."

"George Wickham?"

She nodded silently and folded her gloves together. "Your closest friend, I take it. I found him quite engaging."

"Engaging or not, I would have you know that he is not a guest whose company I permit here. I would encourage you to take a similar stance at Corbett."

"Interesting, as I just saw him riding away when I came up."

"A matter of business, but it is at an end. He is not welcome again."

She tilted her head and studied him with those liquid eyes, her lips softly parted. "I do wonder, Mr Darcy, what could have been so objectionable about the man that you forbid his presence? You believe him so odious that you brought me in to prevent his inheriting, but I found his manners perfectly engaging. I start to think I ought to feel badly for receiving what ought to have gone to another."

He frowned and made a formal bow. "I have no doubts that my sister is anxious for your safe return. I shall see you at dinner, Mrs Wickham." He turned on his heel and closed the door to his study, ignoring the bemused look in those dark eyes when he walked away from her.

May 1813

I T WAS RARE THAT Georgiana wished to go into Lambton. There was little need for her to wander the shops—everything she desired was purchased in London or crafted especially for her by the very finest hands. But, occasionally, Elizabeth would prevail upon Miss Darcy to accompany her into the nearest town merely for the sake of some diversion.

Georgiana Darcy was a friendly soul, but her wealth and status only worsened her innate shyness. The townspeople's eagerness to please Mr Darcy's sister made her less confident, rather than more so. However, and in great part due to Elizabeth's own growing familiarity with the town, Georgiana had stumbled upon one or two establishments in which she felt welcome without feeling conspicuous.

One such place was the bookshop where the proprietor would stand aside for an hour to suggest new delights to suit the ladies' fancies. On these occasions, Georgiana would happily purchase anything he advised for herself, and never failed to secure another book for Elizabeth, despite the protestations of the latter.

Another, oddly, was the local coaching inn. The ebb and flow of travellers through the common rooms meant that there were many who did not know Miss Darcy for the princess of the county, and that slight hint of anonymity pleased her. She and Elizabeth occasionally spent the afternoon observing the passing humanity from the relative seclusion of one of the private alcoves. The innkeeper, a respectable man named Samuel Jameson, kept them well supplied with tea and scones and ensured that no one troubled them. The young ladies amused themselves by imagining where a certain businessman was bound, or how long a particular couple had been wed, or the tragic story behind a notable countenance.

One Wednesday afternoon, a woman entered in a state of agitation and called for the proprietor. This caught Elizabeth's notice, for the woman appeared to be attired as a lady of leisure, but she was not accompanied by any husband or servant. Thinking she had discovered a person of interest, Elizabeth nudged Georgiana and they quietly witnessed the unfolding conversation.

"Samuel," the woman cried, "the man you sent gave a most alarming report! Do you truly refuse to help me?"

The innkeeper wiped his hands and made a silencing gesture. "Come by later. My wife can speak with you."

"I do not want that silly wife of yours. She hasn't two wits to rub together. What is the meaning of this?"

He leaned close to the woman and spoke in tones low enough that Elizabeth and Georgiana, across the room, could not hear. His embarrassment and desire to send her away were perfectly clear, but the more he tried to divert her, the more rooted she seemed to be to her spot.

"I think she must be his lover," whispered Georgiana.

"Goodness, what sort of novels are you reading?" Elizabeth whispered back. "That sounds more like Kitty's sort of entertainment."

"But see how familiar they are? They must be..." Georgiana reddened. "You know."

"Or they could simply be neighbours or relatives."

"Samuel," the woman lamented at last, "you are of positively no use! I can see that I will have to solve this trouble on my own."

"Do as you will, Isabella," he grumbled as he turned away. "You never would listen."

"See?" Georgiana hissed.

Elizabeth silenced Georgiana, for at that moment the woman had turned round and her eyes fell on them. She looked curious, then thoughtful, and then she boldly approached.

"I beg your pardon," she inquired sweetly, "but would you be Miss Georgiana Darcy and Mrs Elizabeth Wickham?"

They glanced at each other—Georgiana in fear, Elizabeth in confusion. "Those are our names," Georgiana answered hesitantly.

"Oh—" the newcomer rolled her eyes and offered a gentle smile. "Forgive my impertinence in addressing you, but it has been some while that I have greatly desired to meet you."

Georgiana blinked. "Me?"

"No—I beg your pardon again. Her." The woman nodded toward Elizabeth. "My name is Isabella Godfrey—Samuel Jameson here is my brother. I have heard much of the new mistress of Corbett Lodge."

"Godfrey..." Elizabeth repeated slowly. "Why, yes, I have heard your name. It is a pleasure to meet you, madam."

"We have a mutual friend," Mrs Godfrey continued. "I understand you have made the acquaintance of your brother-in-law, Mr George Wickham?" At Elizabeth's concession, she went on. "I knew Mr Wickham when he was but a lad. My husband—God rest his soul—used to have a fine apple orchard, and the dear boy was forever jumping the fence and pilfering the very best apples until one day we caught him and made him to come in like an honest lad and sit at table." A warmth had kindled in Mrs Godfrey's face as she relived what seemed to be a pleasant memory.

Georgiana had turned very red at all this account, and Elizabeth wondered briefly at it, but was more intrigued by the new acquaintance before her. "That is a very kind response to youthful indiscretions," she replied.

"Oh! One could not help but be kind to George. The poor lad had a hard time of it with his elder brother always taking advantage of him. You know how boys often are!"

Elizabeth shifted uncomfortably. "I am sorry to say that I know very little of the family history."

"My dear lady," Mrs Godfrey laughed, "pray, do not interpret my words as any slight against you on account of your departed husband. We all do as we must, and I say thank heaven that Corbett Lodge is become a respectable place again. It is a pity that poor George shall not have what he expected, but if not he, then what a mercy that it fell to a fine woman like yourself."

Georgiana was looking at the floor now, and Elizabeth could even see that her shoulders had begun to hunch. She looked questioningly at her friend, but then returned her attention to Mrs Godfrey. "Forgive me for asking, but do you... are Mr Wickham's prospects much harmed?"

Mrs Godfrey's expression sobered. "Forever ruined, I should say. I regret to tell you that the poor man seems to have made an enemy of a rather powerful gentleman, though he confessed to me he is quite at a loss as to how. And, despite all hope to the contrary, that person was pleased to see him destitute. Oh, but do not look so downcast yourself, Mrs Wickham!" she interjected at Elizabeth's turn of countenance. "You could have known none of this, and I have heard enough fine and noble things of your character to think very well of how matters came about for you. I am certain you are just as deserving, and perhaps more so. Such a pleasure it gave me when I heard how wonderfully you care for your widowed mother and sisters! 'There, Isabella,' I said to myself, 'there is a lady you ought to meet,' and I am very glad I have done so."

"I am honoured," Elizabeth answered, but in a numb, automatic sort of speech.

"All the honour is mine, I assure you. But there! I had a rather troublesome matter to address, so I must away. I understand it would be difficult to call on you at Corbett, but if you are ever near East Orchards, I should be delighted to receive you. Good day, Mrs Wickham, Miss Darcy."

"Good day," Elizabeth repeated.

Georgiana remained silent.

Seven

"ᴀɴᴅ ᴛʜɪꜱ ɪꜱ ᴛʜᴇ last of the accounts?" Darcy asked Daniels, his steward. His desk was littered from a long afternoon of the most wearisome sort of business—that of patching up the sorry affairs of another.

"Yes, Mr Darcy. We have made a thorough search, and no other can make any claims—of paternity or debt or otherwise—of Mr Bernard Wickham."

Darcy sighed. "So end it. A good thing, too, for I doubt my coffers could have endured another decade of his debauchery."

"With all due respect, Mr Darcy, there was never any requirement for you to see it all attended to."

"There was—a promise of sorts. Moreover..." He allowed the thought to drift as he penned the final signature. Daniels sat patiently while he sanded the page, folded the directive, and stamped it with his signet ring. Darcy paused as he handed the sealed missive back to his steward. "I dislike seeing innocents harmed by a rogue."

"And that is why it is a privilege to work for you, sir," Daniels answered in a curiously husky tone.

Darcy dismissed the compliment with a brusque wave of his hand. "Have we any other business this afternoon?"

"Only if you wish to look over some of your investments, sir. There are also the latest foals born, a report on the lambs—"

"Tomorrow, Daniels." Darcy rose from his desk and subtly flexed his tired calves behind the desk.

"Very good, sir. I am at your leisure."

After Daniels had gone, Darcy walked to the hearth and at last gave in to the urge to stretch his shoulders, roll his taut neck, and draw several deep breaths. Long and tedious work it had been, but Bernard Wickham and his affairs were now behind him. Save for the problem of his "widow." But he had a plan there, provided that the lady was willing to heed his advice... and he could manage to carry it off.

"William?" The door to his study cracked, and Georgiana's voice sounded small and fragile.

He turned and gestured for her to enter. "What is the trouble, Georgiana?"

She came, her hands clasped tightly before her, and her steps shortened. "William, something dreadful happened in Lambton today."

Instantly his eyes went to the door, and his body tensed. "Where is Mrs Wickham? She is not harmed in some way? Has someone offended her?"

"No, quite the opposite. We met a woman today... oh, it is in every way distressing!" She covered her mouth with the tips of her fingers and quelled a few hasty breaths before continuing. "Do you know a Mrs Isabella Godfrey?"

Darcy's brow furrowed in thought. "I am not familiar with the name."

"Are you certain?" Georgiana pressed. "She claims to be a widow, and sister to Mr Jameson at the inn. She told us she resides at East Orchards, and made it sound as if she had always lived there."

He narrowed his eyes. "The only one I recall who could possibly make such claims is... but no, I thought she died or fell to ruin years ago."

Georgiana stepped closer. "Who?"

"Why do you wish to know? This must have been some peculiar encounter."

"It was. William, she claims a special fondness for George Wickham, and she said she had been longing to meet Elizabeth, as the new mistress of Corbett. She had the oddest things to say about how Mr Wickham was cheated of his inheritance by someone who wished to do him harm, but that it was still a good job that Elizabeth had got it in the end. It was all so fearfully uncomfortable! I simply did not know what to say—I wished to leave, but I could not very well do that."

"Georgiana, tell me everything you recall. Was this a tallish woman, with hair that is more red than brown?"

She nodded. "Yes, that sounds right."

"Expressive features, smiles too often and is somewhat brazen in her approach?"

"Yes, yes, that is her! Do you know her after all?"

He frowned. "No."

"But William! You must know who she is. I think she was quite taken with Elizabeth and begged her to call if she ever could."

His gaze sharpened on his sister. "And what of E—Mrs Wickham? Did she appear equally enamoured by the acquaintance?"

"That is what troubles me, for I could not be sure. Mrs Godfrey was everything pleasant and inviting, and you know, I think Elizabeth still feels somewhat unwelcome here in Derbyshire."

"Has she said that?"

"No, but it is in her manner, do you know? I suppose if I were Bernard's widow and had to hear all the awful things said about him, I would scarcely feel less uncomfortable."

"But back to Mrs Godfrey, did Mrs Wickham appear to credit her words?"

Georgiana shrugged. "Well, why would she not? I wanted to tell Elizabeth all about George Wickham, but I feared to say anything after we came away, for I thought 'What if she discovers the truth about me?' I do not think I could bear for her to hate me, William!"

He reached into his pocket and withdrew a handkerchief for his sister to dab eyes that had swelled with sudden tears. "She would never hate you, but you did right, for I would not have her know all."

Georgiana's lip trembled. "Surely, this is nothing of consequence. You mean to tell me now that I am fretting over nothing, yes? I mean—" her hands twisted together unhappily—"It was just one conversation, and nothing is bound to come of it, right?"

"Of course, my dear," he soothed. "You must not trouble yourself, or your eyes will become swollen and then you truly will have questions to answer from your friend."

She drew a trembling breath and nodded. "Yes, yes, you are right. I will go now. But you will make inquiries after Mrs Godfrey, will you not?"

"Indeed, I will, but I am certain that it was only a passing conversation, as you say. Run along, and I will see you at dinner." He kissed the cheek she lifted to him and stood back as she left the study.

"Isabella Godfrey now, is it?" he murmured to himself. "Let us hope Elizabeth Wickham is made of finer stuff than you were, old girl."

July 1813

E LIZABETH HAD NEVER SEEN a more beautiful sight in all her life than the one that greeted her at her front door. Jane—long-lost Jane, gone these two years to Dorsetshire, now returning to the bosom of her family. Elizabeth raced to her first, nearly sweeping her much taller sister off her feet and twirling her about in transports of joy.

The reunion was boisterous and long, with all six women talking over one another in a frenzy of exultation. There were news to share, gossip to catch up, Lydia's startling new height to marvel over, and every feature and corner of Corbett Lodge to be admired. When they had exhausted their words and hands, they fell to satisfying their stomachs with the bounty from the larder. And the best gift of all—the Darcys had insisted that Elizabeth should remain at least two or three days to welcome her favourite sister, with no concern for rushing back to Pemberley.

"Oh, Lizzy!" Jane draped herself over the sofa, her hand cast over her stomach and her countenance suffused with plenitude for the first time in far too long. "I can only think we have been granted some Providential blessing. I still cannot credit your story!"

"It is true, every word."

Jane lifted her head. "Why, Lizzy, you do not look at all pleased. Do you regret marrying Mr Wickham? Surely the knowledge that his estate would be well cared-for lent him peace in his last days. He must have desired a wife for some reason."

"So I was told, but I am questioning that reason."

Jane straightened, glancing quizzically at their mother. "Oh! Do not listen to Lizzy," scoffed Mrs Bennet. "You know she frets over everything."

"It is far more than 'fretting' to be concerned for the prospects of one who was injured by my gain," Elizabeth replied. "And yes, I am. I have met Mr George Wickham on a few occasions now, and can trace no resemblance to the fearsome creature Mr Darcy sketched for me."

"But your letters told of Mr Darcy's kindness to you," Jane recalled. "How he arranged everything here, cared for his friend's affairs and now acts the gracious employer and generous neighbour. Surely, such a man must have had his reasons for supporting Mr Wickham's decision to marry, rather than permitting the inheritance to pass to his brother."

"Mr Darcy is a person who has some hidden reason for all he does. He rarely speaks more than a sentence or two and never explains his motives, so how am I to understand them? Even kindness can be corrupt, if bestowed for the wrong reasons."

Jane and Mary exchanged a long look, with the latter lifting her shoulders and returning to Fordyce. Jane sighed. "I will trust that so many good things to come into our lives cannot be tainted at their root. When am I to meet this Mr Darcy?"

Elizabeth turned her head at the sound of hoofbeats clattering in the drive. "Right now, it would seem."

It was not merely Mr Darcy. In his company was that Charles Bingley fellow, whose arrival Elizabeth had not known to expect. What inconvenient presumption, and at such a time! As a precaution against unwanted courtliness, Elizabeth kept her greeting to Mr Bingley as short as she could without being uncivil. Oh, he was not a bad sort of man. In fact, she might have heartily liked him, had it not been for Mr Darcy's clear desire that she ought to do so.

Mr Darcy introduced everyone, and Mr Bingley cheerfully fell into conversation with her mother—a thing few gentlemen ever had the temerity or patience for. Elizabeth watched them in a detached fashion, until she sensed Mr Darcy standing at her side.

"Your eldest sister little resembles you," he noted.

She turned a cross look on him. "Is this your typically impolite means of asking if she truly is my sister? I assure you, she is."

"I intended no speculation of the kind, but many families have siblings who, for... various reasons, look quite different from one another."

"Mr Darcy, that statement only affirms to me that you think my sister's birth might have been irregular. Though I have adequate assurances that it was not, it is a terribly coarse observation, and better kept to yourself."

He laughed. "I meant no offense."

"Of course, you did. You delight in espousing opinions designed to provoke."

"And if I do, you never fail to make statements intended either to misdirect the conversation or overtly confront my words."

"Perhaps you could terminate my employment, if my manner is offensive."

Mr Darcy offered an enigmatic smile. "I never said I was offended."

They ceased speaking, and he stood beside her in taut silence, his hands crossed behind his back and his weight balanced forward on his toes. Every so often he would tense, as if thinking of something, and then the notion would pass, and he would stand at ease once more.

"Mr Darcy, had you something to say?" she asked at length. "What can you mean by coming in all this state just to meet my sister?"

"Why, Mrs Wickham, do you not think I would stir myself to greet a new neighbour?"

"No."

His brow wrinkled, and he frowned. "You are correct, I suppose."

"And if your intent was to bring Mr Bingley to my notice and me to his, you have a rather heavy-handed way of going about it."

"I do not think so. Are you not required by the rules of civility to comport yourself as a widow in mourning while at Pemberley? So much the better for any interested gentleman to meet you here, where you are more at home and such a gentleman might know your family."

"Are you speaking of Mr Bingley or yourself?"

Mr Darcy's complexion changed hues—the first she had ever seen him do so. "Myself! That is a curious question to ask, Mrs Wickham."

"Is it? For I am hardly away half a day, but you do not casually ride in this direction."

He blinked and stared across the room. "Merely surveying the drainage from the neighbouring fields, as I do each week at this time of year. And inspecting the flocks, of course."

"You are watching me."

"Indeed not, madam!" He laughed consciously. "What, do you think I have little better to do than to spy on those in my employ whenever they return to their homes?"

She sighed. "Mr Darcy, if you have concerns that I might behave in a manner unbecoming to my post, why do you not speak to me of it?"

"You mistake me, Mrs Wickham. Your name aside—for I suppose you cannot help it that you wed a blackguard—there is no disrepute to be found in you."

"Then you are looking in on the management of the house? May I remind you, sir, that you nearly forced me to accept this duty, and you no longer have the right to express doubt in my abilities—or my mother's, as she acts as mistress while I am away. You do recall that she was mistress of a larger house for twenty years and knows what she is about?"

"Why do you presume that I do anything but what I profess? Can a man not ride out among his neighbours?" Mr Darcy's ears were red at the tips and he was making a point of looking only at Mr Bingley... who had fallen into animated conversation with Jane. Mr Darcy's brow darkened, and he developed a positive frown.

Elizabeth suppressed a smile. "It is a pity."

"I beg your pardon?"

"Oh! Only that you went to all that trouble to make Mr Bingley and me like each other, but he is even less cooperative than I am."

Mr Darcy glanced down at her. "Your sister is handsome, but Bingley is no fool. I hope you will both see the sense of it in time."

Mr Bingley and Jane both burst into a laugh at some silliness, and the gentleman was leaning far closer than a first acquaintance typically permitted.

"Did you ever think, Mr Darcy, that perhaps you are not always right?" Elizabeth asked smugly.

"Never."

Eight

OVER THE NEXT TWO days, Bingley spoke of little else. Jane Bennet was an angel. Jane Bennet had a heart of gold to take a governess' position to help her family. Jane Bennet's honour was unimpeachable, her smile radiant like the sun, and her sweetness unparalleled in all the earth.

Darcy thought rather that the woman was too sweet, in the way of a sugary bun where the salt has been forgotten and there is nothing but the cloying, tooth-ache-inducing stickiness that makes the head spin. And she smiled altogether too much.

"But would not you smile, if you had been gone from your family two years and now suddenly returned under wondrous circumstances?" Bingley protested. "Surely, even you would beam from ear to ear."

Darcy preferred not to think on it, on the chance that he might have to reconsider. "There is nothing objectionable in the lady," he conceded. "She would do handsomely for a tradesman or even a modest gentleman, but for you—"

"Why one sister over the other?" Bingley challenged. "They are both of the same lineage, the same circumstances. Both took positions for work."

"But both are not mistress of their own estate, modest as it is. As you have been wishing to purchase anyway, this satisfies both your desire to secure property and a capable bride. Corbett is too small for your station, but you could always sell it and buy something finer, or perhaps keep it for your second son."

"Say what you will, Darcy," Bingley said with a laugh, "but I will declare Jane Bennet a sweet girl and I should like to know her better."

Darcy hid his chagrin. "You ought to take pains to know Mrs Wickham while you are at it. She is not normally so acerbic as she was yesterday. Rather, she is a lady of a quick wit who objects to being manipulated but can readily be brought to see reason when it is directly before her."

"Why, Darcy, she sounds absolutely… indeed!" Bingley mused as his eyes lit up. "Truly, I have just had the most capital idea, and I daresay it would suit everyone. Why ever do you not pursue the lady?"

"I! Pursue Mrs Wickham? Impossible."

"Why not? You told me once yourself that Georgiana is coming out next autumn and would do better with a sister-in-law than a companion. It seems to me you might have found both in the same woman."

Darcy scowled at the simplistic notion. "Even if I did not find it distasteful to court a woman presently in my employ, there are other reasons."

"Oh," Bingley scoffed, "yes, yes, Pemberley's future mistress must have connections nearly to the Prince himself and a fortune to rival Midas, and—"

"This is true," Darcy interrupted. "Indeed, I wish it was not, but there it is. However, there is yet a more pressing reason I could never take her as my bride. The very reason I coaxed her to wed Bernard in the first place. No. Society's expectations I could thwart if I chose to—heaven knows, my father did—but my honour I cannot sacrifice."

Bingley looked disbelieving. "What honour would you be compromising?"

Darcy shook his head and forced a smile. "Never mind. It is enough to state that even if I desired it—and I do not, to be clear—I could never offer for Mrs Wickham. You, however—"

"Oh, Darcy, let it rest. If I chose Mrs Wickham as you desire, I would still need to wait another seven months before she can wed."

"Six."

"Six, rather. Has it been that long already? But in any case, I have plenty of time to know the whole family better. And what of you? You did not go to Rosings this spring with Colonel Fitzwilliam."

"No."

Bingley watched him with a bemused smile and lifted a drink to his mouth. "That was a rather short answer," he observed after a moment.

"A short answer for a clear solution. Lady Catherine threatened to sever ties if I did not take Anne back. As if I would have taken her in the first place! I am sorry for my cousin, but not that sorry."

"A pity," Bingley lamented with no hint of sincerity in his voice. "For if you had taken Anne, you would not now be tempted to press Mrs Wickham off on another before you succumbed to her charms yourself."

Darcy shot his friend a caustic look. "Have you not a horse to ride or a lady to court?"

Bingley rose from his chair with a chortle. "Two ladies, it would seem—one to please myself and the other to please you. Do you know, I might just ignore your advice when the time comes. I daresay that would be a first." He left his glass on a side table and paused before going.

"Darcy, I know you have never taken my advice—as if I had any words of wisdom to offer you! But consider—a man is bound to his wife for a very long time. Would it not be preferable to choose a lady in whose company you can delight for the rest of your years?" He gave a strange little smile, then left Darcy alone.

A lady in whose company he could delight.

Yes, that would be ideal. Darcy wandered to the window and pressed his forearm against the glass, gazing out. Summer was in full bloom now, with the grass thick and tall over the distant meadow and the heady fragrance from the gardens tempting him each time he stepped out of doors. And the flowers were not the only thing tempting him.

There she was, coming up the garden walk, prompt and faithful after her promised two days away. There was something in her he could not resist. He owned it fully. A sharpness, a high and fine edge he found exhilarating to walk. And yet, if a man slipped from the precipice, he could be assured of a gentle landing place. Darcy sighed and felt a small ache rip into the fabric of his heart.

Six months before she could marry again, and she would be beyond his reach. Six months of her continued presence in his home, her voice filling his ears and her intelligence to hone his.

They would be the longest six months in all his life.

"**G**OOD AFTERNOON, SISTER ELIZABETH!"

Elizabeth raised her bonnet from the path. Another Sunday afternoon was gone, and she was setting out again for Miss Darcy's company. Odd, how she dreaded the parting from her family's embrace, but the moment her hand touched the gate latch, she felt only pleasure in returning to her friend.

This day, she had scarcely started up the lane when George Wickham appeared mounted to her right. He touched his hat at her recognition and swung to the ground with a wrapped parcel in his hand.

"Good afternoon to you, sir," she greeted him. "We have not seen you in some weeks."

"Unforgivable and, yet unavoidable," he replied with a bow. "In penance, I bring you a gift from an old friend. You recall how I recommended Mrs Brown's cooking to you, I hope? I was just coming from Lambton and happened upon her. When I told her I was riding this way in hopes of giving you my salutations, she pressed me to bring this. I trust it will not be unwelcome." He presented his parcel and unwrapped it just enough to give Elizabeth a delicious whiff of the spiced rum cake.

"How very kind of her! I wish I had some prior acquaintance with her. You must give her our thanks."

"I have already done so, for I knew you would wish me to. Shall we take it back to the house?" he asked with a tip of his head.

Elizabeth looked regretfully back. "I wish I could, but if I did, I should be late in returning to Miss Darcy."

"Oh! Miss Darcy would not mind, particularly if you told her the cause."

"But I would, for I have given my solemn pledge to be faithful in my duties to her. As I am quite dependent upon others when they give their word, so I shall not break mine. I am afraid it is dreadfully unneighbourly, but I must ask you to speak with Millie, the kitchen maid. She is just there going out to the hens—you can see her now."

"Well, then! I see I shall have to come much earlier in the day if I wish to call properly on my sister-in-law. But do not think of it, for I quite understand your predicament. Perhaps I shall walk with you as far as the field, then turn back with my gift."

She nodded her permission, and they started off. "I wonder if you have heard," she asked, "but I had the pleasure of meeting Mrs Godfrey."

"I did hear. She is a pleasant soul, is she not? Very kind to me as a lad, and a straight-faced, honest lady if ever I knew one. Some might find her off-putting, but she is not afraid to call out the powerful or lift the heads of the weak. She is the only lady I have found who so merits my whole esteem."

"That is generous praise indeed, and a thing we ought all to aspire to. She said something rather curious about you making an enemy, and naturally I assumed she referred to Mr Darcy, as it seems you two are not friends."

He smiled. "Sister Elizabeth, I believe I have found yet a second lady deserving of my regard. I will tell you honestly, but I would caution you to guard your tongue when others are about. Derbyshire is full of Darcy's people."

"You make it sound as if we are at war and he is the enemy camp!"

"It is very like that," he replied soberly. "I suppose Darcy told you that my brother had little fondness for me?"

"He did say... something of the kind," Elizabeth answered cautiously.

"I should have thought so. It is true—Bernard and I were never friendly as brothers ought to be. The source of our strife was not clear to all, for what brothers do not disagree on occasion? But, you see, Bernard and I were not truly brothers."

Elizabeth gasped. "You were not!"

"Oh, in the legal sense, of course we were. My father acknowledged us both and none can contest that. Mr Darcy the elder had his own solicitor on the task, so you can be sure it was done proper. But blood? We shared not a drop. Bernard, well, he always hated me for how much better our parents loved me while he had no notice from his natural father."

"And he did not know who it was?"

Mr Wickham scoffed. "No one 'knew,' so the story goes. But when George Darcy bestowed Corbett Lodge on my father for his many years of faithful service, Bernard drew his own conclusions. I am sure you can well imagine. My father vehemently denied to both of us that George Darcy could have been Bernard's father, and that good and worthy gentleman said much the same on his deathbed. Corbett was not some recompense to the natural son of a wealthy man—it was truly meant to go to my father and his heirs. Unfortunately—" Here, he sighed quietly. "Bernard was the eldest. And so, here we are."

Elizabeth swallowed the knot in her throat. "And now it is forever lost to you, all because of me!"

"My dear sister," he soothed, "pray do not take my words for any bitterness of spirit. No, I insist, put away your tears for me! Having you for a relation is blessing enough, for you have done what I could never do at that tumbled down abode. Why, have you heard the praise all the tenants have for the wise 'Widow Wickham?' Indeed, it is well that one such as you has been entrusted with its care."

"But you would have done as well or better," she protested. "It ought rightfully to have been yours and you know every particular of the neighbours and the property."

"Here, now! What sort of talk is this from a lady who is now caring for her entire family by her alliance? No, I cannot in any way begrudge you that. Indeed, I would have made the same decision in your place, so the fault is not yours."

"It was Mr Darcy who insisted upon it," Elizabeth muttered in some frustration. "It was he who said—"

"My dear sister," Mr Wickham laughed, "we would be here a very long time if you determined to enumerate all Darcy's faults for me. I daresay we all have our share, and perhaps a man with so many blessings has even more flaws than most. But I tell you what would cheer my heart better than to hear you abuse a fellow who is decent enough, in his way. Truly, it would be just the sort of gesture that a noble and generous woman would think of—passing on the bounty, you could say."

She raised her brows. "Yes?"

"Had you ever considered what would become of Corbett if you remarried? I daresay your husband would count it among his possessions and that would be the end of it. He might even sell it, as I suspect would be the case. But what of a permanent home for your mother and sisters?"

Elizabeth frowned down at the path. "What do you mean?"

"Oh, nothing really, it was just a trifling thought. I am sure you would wish to use the estate as your dowry to make a fine match, and for that I could not blame you."

"I think you mistake me and all my motives if you believe that."

He smiled. "No. I have not mistaken you. Well, then my advice is to deed the estate to your mother."

"My mother!"

He shrugged. "Or one of your younger sisters. Yes, that might do better, for they will see to her care longer than she will see to theirs."

"But how could I?" she objected. "Would it even be legal?"

"Oh, legal, certainly. It is yours in every respect, with no entail to fear. You could ask a solicitor for his advice, though I do not recommend using Darcy's man. The old boy might disapprove, for I think he intends you and the estate for one of his friends."

"He does," she answered with a scowl. "My uncle is an attorney in Meryton. Perhaps I will write to him."

"An excellent notion. And as we are now nearing Pemberley's lands, I will bid you a good afternoon and return this rum cake to your family. A pleasant walk, Sister."

Elizabeth watched him mount and ride away, then turned to face Pemberley. And its master.

Nine

"No, Darcy, my mind is quite made up. Mrs Wickham is a charming woman, but she would not suit me." Charles Bingley stopped at the head of the billiards table, cue in hand. He straightened his back and made a hesitant posture that was likely meant to appear determined and dared to meet Darcy's gaze.

"Nonsense! She is precisely the sort of woman you want. Capable and intelligent—she would keep you directed. You will wish for such a wife when you purchase your own house."

"No, it is no good, Darcy. I've quite fallen for Miss Bennet, and is she not also a gentleman's daughter who was taught from her infancy to be mistress of a house?"

"A small house," Darcy clarified. "I have made inquiries, and the Bennets' share was not a large one. However, Mrs Wickham has the rare capacity to stretch beyond her early training."

"But Miss Bennet has my heart, and she is in no way deficient."

Darcy snorted. "You would run yourselves into debt within a twelvemonth by letting every servant and shopkeeper cheat you."

Bingley grinned. "Better to endure poverty with such a woman than a king's treasure without her. I am sorry, Darcy, but for this once, I cannot heed your advice. I have had three weeks now to know them both, and though that may not be long, I am quite determined. I mean to make her an offer before I return to London."

Darcy bent over the table to make another shot, shaking his head all the while. "Why such a rush? At least let it go until you come back again. The lady might well forget you, and if she did, you would be at no loss."

"Miss Bennet would never!"

The billiards cracked, and Darcy straightened. "If you are so sure of her, then what harm in waiting? Come back again in September for the shooting, and then you will know for certain what sort of woman you would take to wife."

Bingley twisted the chalk over the end of his cue with somewhat more force than necessary. His face contorted in an agony of disappointment and better judgment. "Very well."

B INGLEY DEPARTED THE FOLLOWING day, and as far as Darcy knew, he did not detour to Corbett Lodge before driving south. The house seemed quiet without him, for the man was like a great leaping hound, always exulting over life and simple pleasures. In his absence, Darcy's own more introspective spirits felt withdrawn and languishing. Even Georgiana appeared dull.

He could not decide about Mrs Wickham.

She seemed not to care, and even went about her days in precisely the same manner as before. He was uncertain whether to be relieved or disappointed in this, and watched her all the more carefully to detect some disturbance of mind. And then, he saw it. A melancholy sigh in an odd moment; a wistful watching out the window when no one was expected; a curious frown upon her brow when she was at her needlework.

"You are very quiet this evening, Mrs Wickham," he observed one night, about a fortnight after Bingley's departure. "I hope your family are well."

She looked up, and her expression smoothed. "I thank you, yes. My mother sent over a note that my sister wished for some cordial to cheer her, for her spirits are low."

"Truly? I hope you applied to Mrs Reynolds. She would be pleased to send some to her."

"I have, thank you." She bowed her head again over her needlework, and that was the end of the conversation.

August 1813

T HREE WEEKS AFTER BINGLEY'S departure, Darcy was out taking the air in the garden when he happened upon her alone. She was walking without her bonnet and spencer, her dark hair shining in the sunlight and the shadowy cut of her figure softly displayed through the sheer fabric of her summer gown.

They both stopped abruptly upon encountering one another, and Darcy felt an uncommon flush through his centre. Devil take it, but she was a stunning creature, and all the more so because she seemed perfectly unaware of it. He bowed quickly to hide the sudden rush of heat to his face.

"I beg your pardon, sir. I will not disturb your constitutional." She curtsied and began to turn away, but he stopped her.

"In fact, I would enjoy the company, madam."

She turned back without a word and fell into step beside him. Darcy watched her surreptitiously for several paces but could not determine what to say.

"I believe we must have some conversation, sir," she said after some minutes.

"Must we?"

"It is the established convention when one requests another's company. It is therefore left to the requestor to initiate said conversation."

He allowed a half smile. "What would you like to speak of?"

She gestured to the manicured hedges. "You could regale me with tales of your great-great-grandfathers all the way to Cromwell who must have designed the opulent splendour we see around us."

"If I wished to be bored to the point of tears."

"Why, then, you could identify for me rose varieties that I know perfectly well, but you know I will listen politely and feign ignorance because that is my part in the conversation."

Darcy clasped his hands behind his back and tried not to allow his amusement to show. "I despise flowers," he lied. "Sugary, fragrant things—they give me the head-ache."

"Then perhaps we may speak of Miss Darcy and her anticipation of her coming out. I understand her aunt, Lady Matlock, is to sponsor her?"

"And Lady Matlock is the one to whom you should apply for intelligence on the matter. My only understanding of the process is that I am to pay a vast sum for the pleasure of recruiting some naif to take away my only sister and her dowry."

"Then perhaps a matter dearer to my own heart?" she suggested.

"Have you such?"

"What person does not?" she asked with a faint edge to her voice.

"Mrs Wickham, any cares of yours are also my own," he replied with what he hoped was more gallantry than boorishness.

She stopped and turned to him. "Let us speak of Corbett Lodge."

"Speak of it? Whatever for? But, very well. It is a moderately sized house made of stone, approximately one hundred fifteen years old, settled in a pleasant valley with atrocious soil and poor drainage. It makes hardly enough to sustain itself in rents and will need further repairs to the chimney before winter if your family are not to die of asphyxiation."

"So, as you once said to me, the house is no gift? Would you go so far as to say that it is more of a curse, sir?"

"A curse! No, far from it. I fancy it is a good deal finer than what many call their abode."

"Then I have another question for you, sir. What manner of offense must a person commit to be considered undeserving of the inheritance that had been designed for him?"

Darcy narrowed his eyes. "If you are now inquiring about the person I believe you to be, what makes you think there was only one offense?"

"Because I cannot imagine how there could be more—or, rather, I do not understand how his crimes could be sufficient for you to be justified in all your actions. I would ask you to enlighten me, for you must know it has been a burden to my conscience."

He gazed down at her, admiring the fire that had kindled to life in those dark, bright eyes. If he continued so, without speaking something of sense, he was in very great danger of his tongue running on without his head. He cleared his throat briefly.

"It is a credit to you that you could feel thus," he began, "but in matters of virtue, there is no question. George Wickham is all shine and appeal, but he is bankrupt in essentials."

She tilted her head, and Darcy's eye was captured by the way the light shafted off her cheekbones. Several old French phrases teased his memory—both oaths and endearments, and a pounding almost-nausea passed through his being. Un trésor...

"Mr Darcy, thus far you have only assured me in the blandest of terms. If you truly expect me to look myself in the mirror and sleep the sleep of the just, I must know that I have not been used in some nefarious way to harm an innocent man."

"Harm an innocent! Yes, George Wickham knows all about such things."

"By his account, yes!" she answered with energy. "What was his crime? Bringing baked goods to a widow? Standing aside for another's happiness?"

Darcy's hands had fallen to his sides now, and his chest was strangely tight. "Deeds such as his are not fit for the ears of a maiden," he replied flatly.

"Ah, but Mr Darcy, do you forget that in the eyes of the world, I am a widow? I have no dignity, no innocence, no reputation to risk."

He set his teeth and looked beyond her, merely to keep himself from falling the dazzled victim of the fire in those glorious eyes. Merveilleuse... "It is not merely your innocence I would protect," he growled.

She drew a steadying breath, visibly counting before she responded. "Is it true that Bernard Wickham was not the natural son of his father?"

Darcy stared. "He told you this? And I suppose he meant to engage your sympathies? The poor blighted younger son, is that what he tickled your ears with?"

"I am no foolish girl," she retorted hotly. "I do not fall easily to flattery, and I resent the implication that I would mindlessly heed empty words."

"If you listen to George Wickham, that is all you will hear."

"Then try me." She crossed her arms. "I beseech you."

Darcy gazed down at her—the righteous indignation simmering in her vibrant figure, the sharp, furious words ready to pierce him should he err in his next phrase. His very body ached. Sacré bleu...

"Mr Darcy," she sighed impatiently, "perhaps I shall ask another way. Why did you intend for me to marry Mr Bingley when my mourning is complete?"

"I thought it was obvious. He is a good and noble man and would make a fine husband. You would have answered his needs in every way—it was a perfect notion."

"Until he announced his preference for my sister."

Darcy blinked. "You are making assumptions."

"I have it from Mr Bingley himself. He told me as much just before he departed—and also that you had imposed upon him to defer his offer. I cannot think why you would have done so, unless you intended to pressure him into changing his mind."

"Bingley is often heedless," he retorted. "Imprudent. I only wished for him to consider all the options. A marriage to you instead would—"

"Would what?" she interrupted. "Break my sister's heart? Set your friend up with what ought rightly to have belonged to another? That is the root of it, is it not, Mr Darcy? You planned all along to use me to divert a neighbouring estate to a man you liked better than the rightful heir."

"You are mistaken!" he cried impetuously.

"Am I? How? Why else would you be so insistent upon me marrying Mr Bingley?" She set her hands at the curve of her waist, leaning forward until she was glaring directly into his face. Darcy felt a great seizure in his chest, a final battle waged and lost. Merde.

Whatever sense had remained in his head after meeting her evaporated, to be replaced by one blinding instant of passion—stinging relief in the truth spoken, and then burning regret at the consequences.

"Because if Bingley married you," he snapped, "then I would not be so tempted to win you for myself!"

H E DID NOT... ELIZABETH cringed and shook herself. He did not just say what she thought she heard... did he?

But the faintly greenish tinge to his complexion, the guilty look in his dark eyes, and the way he was shrinking back from his own words told the truth. Impossible! She swallowed hastily and looked from right to left, desperately hoping no other could have overheard his outburst.

He was grimacing, closing his eyes and drawing ragged breaths as he extended his hand to her. "Good lord," he whispered. "I never meant to confess it."

"You have confessed nothing," she answered quickly. "Look! No harm done—nothing to be remembered. Let it all be forgotten, shall we?" She turned in a rush and would have hurried from the garden, but her hand snagged on his.

"Please, Mrs Wickham—damnation, I cannot call you that name! Elizabeth—Elizabeth, please, hear me a moment," he begged.

He still held her hand, she did not pull it from his, but she continued backing away. "What is there to hear? No, sir, I cannot! I—I am employed in your household!"

His chest rose, and he dropped her hand. "You are perfectly right. F-forgive me." His face clouded with baffled hurt, and he began to turn away in something of a stupor.

Elizabeth cast her gaze upward and prayed for calm. It had never happened.

"Elizabeth!" He had turned back and now stood close—so close she could see the fine weave of his waistcoat and the heartbeat pulsing at his throat. "There is something you must hear."

She shook her head. "You have told me far more than I ever wished to know."

"Not that. I—" He winced, even put his gloved knuckles to his mouth before continuing. "There is more. I would not have you think that pride of position would prevent me—"

"Pray, sir, desist!" she interrupted. "From our very first meeting, you impressed me with your arrogance and conceit. You have coerced, you have manipulated, you have played me for a fool. Every kindness and every consideration shown my family, they were all pawns in some elaborate game! Your motives are now clear to me, sir, and I wish to heaven I had never been the recipient of your 'goodwill.'"

Anger flared in his cheeks. "Mrs Wickham, have a care! You do not know of what you speak."

"If I do not, can I be faulted? I have been chosen seemingly at random and fattened like a Christmas goose, unsuspecting that my true purpose was to grace some other's table. Or his bed! Thank heaven Mr Bingley has more character than—"

"Elizabeth Bennet!" he hissed between his teeth. "If that is the name to which you will answer, by whatever means I must, I will make myself heard!"

She froze at the name of her youth, the name she had lost the day she met him. A lump in her throat... no, it was the threat of tears. She clenched her eyes before they could flood and held up a staying hand. "I can bear no more, sir," she said with a cracking voice. "Pray—let me to the house. I will pack my things at once."

"And go where? Impossible! As you have said before, our... connection, such as it is, it not so readily severed."

"And yet, sever it I must! Send me whatever papers necessary. I will deed Corbett Lodge to the first person to appear worthy, and I will take my mother and sisters back to Meryton. I—I am very sorry for Miss Darcy." These last words were spoken in a hoarse whisper as the tears fell to scald her cheeks. She looked away, miserably wiping her eyes with her fingertips.

"No, Mrs Wickham," he answered gently. "I will go. Of the two of us, yours is the only presence that is indispensable here just now."

Elizabeth looked up, but he was already walking away from her. "Do not be ridiculous, Mr Darcy!" she protested. "You cannot simply leave Pemberley and your sister!"

He turned back for a moment. He said nothing, but the emptiness in his eyes... heaven have mercy, it rent something within her own heart. A few measured blinks, an indrawn breath, and then his face closed again. With a shake of his head, he took his leave.

Elizabeth sagged back against the prickling hedge, not even mindful of how the thorns tore at her gown and tender skin. Exhaustion and sheer physical agony, as pure and raw as any she had ever known, threatened to render her insensible. Somehow, she fumbled her way back to the house with a murmured excuse to the footman that she was indisposed and could not join Miss Darcy for tea. To drown herself in the great copper bathtub, to hide away under her blankets, to never see or speak to another person until this mysterious ache had vanished, these were her only hopes for comfort.

There was no solace to be had.

Ten

Elizabeth awoke the next morning far later than was her wont and rubbed sleep-deprived eyes against the sunlight filtering through the drapes. She had made up her mind—she would tell Miss Darcy that she could not remain. And then she would have to address her mother and sisters and tell them they must return to Aunt and Uncle Philips while she sought new work. The only trouble was that she had not the strength even to rise from the bed.

A curious rustling caused her to lift her head, and she discovered one of Pemberley's maids setting up a tea cart. "What is this?"

The maid started, then bobbed a quick curtsy. "The master said before he left that you were feeling poorly, ma'am. Miss Darcy asked me to bring this up."

Elizabeth blinked, trying to focus her dry eyes. "The master left?"

"Yes, ma'am. Gone to London, he said. He left instructions for you. Will you take your tea now, or shall I call for Nancy to dress you?"

Elizabeth shook her head. "Tea now would be lovely. You may go, Sarah."

"Ma'am," the girl answered with another dip of her head.

Elizabeth's limbs now tingled with urgency, and she moved quickly to the tea cart. Sarah had prepared the first cup for her, and thoughtlessly she caught it up. Her real object was the folded note beside it, and she hurried with both to the window seat. In the author's typical fashion, the note contained no salutation and immediately embarked upon his purpose.

> *Be not alarmed, madam, that this note will contain any renewal of the intimacies I presumed upon yesterday. Two offences of the most grievous nature have been laid at my feet, and*

I must be allowed to answer them by whatever means I may.

The first, that I wilfully intervened in another man's inheritance to suit my own pleasures, is a crime to which, if true, you ought rightly to have responded as you did. It is a travesty, and no man could be absolved of presuming so.

The second, that of misleading and taking advantage of an honourable lady and attempting to force her into a match against her choosing to suit my own ends, is equally heinous, and yet I cannot so easily find myself innocent. I will address this matter first.

Within the first moments of our meeting, I was struck by your intelligence, your dignity, and the apparent strength with which you had endured your prior circumstances. Your bearing and manner, and also your obvious education, were clearly the product of a genteel upbringing, but to these you added yet another virtue. You knew the meaning of hardship, of deprivation, and above all, gentleness. You may understand why I found these qualities essential to the situation after I have said all.

If I have pressured you to accept circumstances that you now regret, I can only beg your forgiveness. As you found at first, the opportunity to shelter a family, restore lands in need of stewardship, and to provide an exemplary woman to guide and befriend my younger sister were all answered in the same moment. If my motives were impure, I can at least say they were not without fruit.

My desire to aid Bernard Wickham in his quest for a wife was two-fold. The first need you met with your able management of the property, for if you had not been aware before, the tenant lands as well as the house had been allowed to deteriorate. Though you could not provide the means of repair, what you did offer was something more vital. You cared for the tenants out of your bounty. I heard regular reports of you or someone acting upon your direction taking baskets to the sick or helping to order the accounts that had been in disarray. This was my hope and, dare I say it, I am proud to have had a hand in bringing it about.

The second reason, and the only which mattered to Bernard, was as you have guessed. It was insupportable that the estate should pass to George Wickham upon the demise of his elder brother.

Bernard and George Wickham were not blood brothers, as you have been told. It is true that Bernard was taken in by his parents and given a name that was not his by birth, and thus I called him by his Christian name. The preference was his own in life, for he knew well that Franklin Wickham was not his natural father and declined to take the name where he could. He believed himself to be sired by my own father, and while he had his health, never ceased to protest that had he not been born on the wrong side of the blanket, Pemberley would have gone to him. This much is not true, but what is true is that Corbett was designed for him on behalf of his natural parent.

Such had been settled in writing at Bernard's birth. As Franklin Wickham had been married five years with no issue before he adopted the child, there was no expectation that any other would inherit it. Bernard was to marry and produce his own heir, but failing that, a codicil in the will besought him, at his discretion, to deed the lands to one precisely such as yourself. The reasons for this peculiar request from the original grantor of the estate were personal, and I shall not expand upon them here. I will only state that the intent of all parties was in every way noble.

Three years after Bernard's birth, Mrs Isabella Wickham quitted the region. None heard from her for considerably more than a year. When she returned, she brought with her a newborn son, ostentatiously christened George in an attempt to win the approval of my father. Mrs Wickham soon left again, and such became her habit, to return after a long absence only to depart once more. This lady you have met, under the guise of Mrs Godfrey. I hope you will be circumspect in your future associations with her.

You may now be asking yourself why I or anyone else would object to the younger son inheriting what the elder left. It is true, Bernard had no heir, and the property would have passed to the crown had no legal transfer occurred and had George Wickham not been in line. As I wrote above, there was an intent in the original bequest that would have been passed over, but even this would have been trifling, had Bernard been satisfied to leave matters as they were. He was not, for reasons of long-standing discord with the prospective heir. Such was his right, and it was my pleasure to concur, for I did not desire the younger brother to be settled so near those under my protection.

I shall now detail something for you which I trust will never reach other ears. The haste I displayed in securing your agreement was only in part due to Bernard's imminent demise. My other cause, even more urgent, was to bring comfort to Georgiana at a vulnerable time. I had taken her from school last summer and sent her to Brighton with another companion by the name of Mrs Younge. While there, Georgiana's letters, which had always overflowed with descriptions of all her doings, became sparse and infrequent. Troubled by this, I took the liberty of calling on her.

I discovered my sister hosting a guest after dinner. When I entered the room, I found her in the midst of a highly provocative waltz, with Mrs Younge accompanying. Her partner was George Wickham, and I discovered that he had been taking her on unescorted outings and staying for long, intimate dinners at home with a dishonest chaperon. I was only just in time to save her virtue, for one of the maids later found a travelling case that he had brought with him upon his arrival.

Georgiana confessed all—she had been persuaded to an elopement, and they intended to take the post-chaise the very next morning to Scotland. At first, she was disinclined to believe what I told her of his character, but when I revealed to her evidence of the many times I had supported his by-blows and found places for the girls he had ruined, she became tearful and de-

spondent. Your arrival just a month after these events was the first thing to cheer her, and she has since continued to improve.

I do not tell you these things to justify all my actions. If I have been wrong in working matters to my design, if it was callous of me to determine my course without consulting the feelings of others, I suffer no misgivings over the outcome. It is with immense pleasure that I have watched your courage rise to each challenge, and I hope that you do not regret coming to Pemberley and to Corbett. Both houses will never again be the same, thanks to you.

I vowed at the opening of this letter to refrain from unsuitable declarations, but if you have read so far, perhaps you will permit me this much. The only thing preventing me from prostrating myself at your feet and beseeching you to grace my side for the rest of my years is a matter of honour. I cannot explain more, and I never shall, but I would move heaven and earth to do away with that one obstacle, if I thought you would ever have me. Perhaps it is well for us both that I know now—you would not.

I intend to remain in London some months, until we can both think on the past without guilt or remorse. We cannot avoid one another's com-

pany forever, but perhaps when we meet again,
it will be as indifferent employer and employee,
or as common neighbours.

God bless you,

Fitzwilliam Darcy

"Elizabeth? Are you well?"

Miss Darcy's muffled voice followed the shy rapping of her knuckles on Elizabeth's door. Quickly, Elizabeth swiped at her eyes and put away Mr Darcy's letter. She had read it through at least four times already and could nearly recite portions of it. Though at first smitten with indignation at the arrogance still resonating in certain of his lines, by the last perusal, the only feeling remaining to her was regret.

"Enter," she called to Miss Darcy, just before draining the last of her cold tea and rising. A maudlin appearance would not do, and mooning over a neglected cup while still in her dressing gown would arouse Miss Darcy's concern more than necessary. She drew back her shoulders and forced a smile as the door opened.

"Oh, I am ever so glad to see you looking bet—" The girl faltered. "What I mean is I had feared you were quite ill indeed. It is surely not so grave as I had imagined, but forgive me for saying it—you look as if something dreadful has happened. What is the matter?"

"Nothing of any concern. A bit of melancholy, that is all."

Miss Darcy's expression altered from worried to sympathetic. "I often feel like that when my brother goes away. I nearly became morose when he told me this morning that he was leaving, but then he reminded me you would be here, and I felt so much better. Is it not wonderful how good company can relieve such dreary feelings?"

Elizabeth's smile became a little warmer, a little less forced. "It is true."

Georgiana sighed. "He was right—he always is, you know. I am glad you are here to cheer me, Elizabeth, but is there some way I can do the same for you? Perhaps you want to spend the day with your family?"

Elizabeth shook her head and felt the final tremors of her anguish shivering away as she took a last, cleansing breath. "No, I thank you, but I would ask you one question."

Miss Darcy tilted her chin, those wide, curious eyes blinking innocently. "Of course."

"Have you ever known your brother to speak anything but the truth?"

The girl sucked in a breath of awe, as if Elizabeth had just profaned some sacrament. "Gracious! Not Fitzwilliam, never. He always speaks the utter truth, even when it pains him. I will confess this to you—pray, do not repeat it to him, for I should not like to remind him of it, but there was a time I doubted him very much. He can seem a little..." Miss Darcy's brow dimpled as she sought the words.

"High-handed? Arrogant? Impossible to comprehend?" Elizabeth supplied.

"But he is truly none of those things. I think rather that he has no patience for foolishness. He has had to deal with much, far more than I know of, I am certain, and he is used to being the only rational person in the room."

"That is a rather conceited perspective!" Elizabeth protested. "You do yourself a disservice if you can excuse him for such a sentiment."

"Oh, I mean when I was a child. He speaks to me differently now, much more like one would expect of an affectionate brother, but it is you he truly respects."

Elizabeth nearly choked and was some seconds in recovering her speech. "Me? He takes every opportunity to provoke me. I should have thought his manner indicative of a tremendous lack of respect, such as he accords everyone beneath himself."

"Not so," Georgiana objected with a vigorous shake of the head. "He treats no one with less than complete regard for their abilities—why, you have seen how he is with Mrs Reynolds and Mr Daniels. But yes, it is different with you. I have never seen him take such delight in bantering with anyone—not since Cousin Richard..." Her face clouded. "Well, perhaps he will set that right one day."

Elizabeth arched a brow and watched for a moment as the girl looked uncomfortably away. "Miss Darcy, shall we adjourn to the instrument to amuse ourselves?"

The girl smiled broadly and clasped her hands before her. "In truth, I thought I would ask you a very great favour, but only if you feel equal to it today. Would you sit for me to paint your portrait?"

"Of course," Elizabeth agreed, with some hesitation in her voice. "But why?"

"Oh! I am trying to improve my skills, and Fitzw…" Her mouth puckered around the last syllables of her brother's name and she faltered, looking apologetically to Elizabeth.

"Do go on," Elizabeth urged. "I am curious what Mr Darcy had to say of my looks. You think perhaps in oil, my features can at last be improved to meet his standards?"

"Nothing of the kind! He said you were very handsome indeed, but that only the most skilled painter could copy the look in your eyes." Georgiana tipped her head this way and that, evaluating Elizabeth's face. "He is right. If I am to have any hope of putting your image down properly, I shall have to pray I can see you the way he does."

Eleven

His London House had never felt so vacant and dull. Darcy had declined three invitations to dinner, for anyone whose company he might have enjoyed were presently in the country. His days were dry and solitary, but he was not so greatly in need of conversation that he wished to endure long evenings of revelry with ladies and gentlemen he cared little for. What he truly lacked, what he most longed for, was someone other than a simpleton or a sycophant to talk to.

After a fortnight of no such luck elsewhere, Darcy found himself knocking at the one door where he might find someone with whom he could truly converse, someone to challenge or even anger him: Richard's flat. Much to his surprise, his cousin even received him.

"To what do I owe the honour?" Richard greeted him with surly irony dripping from his tones.

"Merely paying my respects," Darcy answered. "I did not call when last I was in London."

"I never expected you to this time, either. Oh, yes, Mother told me four days ago that you were in Town. What, did no one else offer to receive you?"

"Quite the contrary. I had hoped to speak with you, but if you still cling to old grievances, I shall depart."

Richard scoffed. "It is not I you must ask, but my wife. She has still not forgiven you for our last meeting."

"For what? Speaking the truth? I said no more than I always say."

"Precisely." Richard shook his head and set his hands at his hips. "I suppose you may as well sit down and have a drink while you are here."

"And I suppose I must thank you for being a gracious host." He accepted both seat and drink from his cousin and paused for a moment before speaking again. "How is Anne?"

Richard shrugged. "You cannot expect a man to truly know how his wife does. Creatures of mystery, they are."

"They needn't be. There is such a thing as a rational woman."

Richard grunted into his glass. "You do not say. Where are these unicorns, the enchanted forests of Derbyshire?"

"Perhaps."

"Then set a trap and put one in a bottle for me," Richard grumbled. "I should like to see such a mythical being with my own eyes."

"I doubt Anne would appreciate the comparison. She would not come off well."

Richard rubbed his forehead with the back of his fist. "Why did you really come today, Darcy? It was not to sing the praises of my bride."

"No." Darcy emptied his glass and set it aside. "I never despised Anne, you know. I never had a high opinion of her—I made no secret of that—but what happened was not entirely her fault."

"I know. It was Lady Catherine's poison and Wickham's golden tongue, but you did blasted little to rectify the matter. You could have told Anne why you would not marry her yourself."

Darcy snorted. "She cannot possibly be that simple. What if she had been with child, as we all suspected at first? Did she truly think I would claim it as my own?"

"You of all men ought to know how to resolve such a dilemma," Richard mumbled. "You manage enough other people's lives."

"And having her marry you was the best choice in every respect—not least because Anne's inheritance allowed you to retire from the military."

"Darcy, I just told you my wife can be irrational, but in this case, I nearly understand her feelings. How long did you leave her with no indication of your intentions? And then after Wickham had misled and used her badly, she looked to you to save her. When you never even answered her letter…"

"I was busy preventing Wickham's next conquest!" Darcy spat. "Pardon me if I cared better for my fifteen-year-old sister than a woman of six and twenty who knew perfectly well what could come of her liaison. She sought to manipulate me in the situation as surely as Wickham did, mark my words—she thinking she could force me into a marriage to preserve the family honour, and he believing I would pay handsomely for his silence. The fool is yourself, for continuing to defend the lady's wounded feelings to me when her own better sense ought to have informed her reality."

"You know Anne better than that by now. She is her mother's daughter in every respect."

"Which is why she persisted so long in her delusions of an engagement to me. I still say a hearty measure of good sense would not serve the lady ill."

"Good sense, you say? Constitutionally impossible, by both breeding and upbringing. In fact, I do not think the woman exists of whom it could be said."

"I heartily disagree. Many are the women who by either prudence or diligence avoid such trials and pitfalls as our cousin had fallen into. And if such a woman does stumble or is dealt a wretched hand, she ought also to have the wits to overcome it."

Richard narrowed his eyes and uncrossed his boots. "By Jove, Darcy, who is she? The unicorn has a name, does she not?"

Darcy looked away. "I speak in general terms, Richard."

"Bollocks. Some faerie has spread her magical dust over your expensive lapels and now you are comparing every woman to her. What is her name?"

"There is no such lady," Darcy retorted testily. "And even if there were, I am no mooncalf or fresh-faced lad."

Richard nodded and pensively drew out a cigar from a box beside his chair. "Of course not. How silly of me. No lady has ever succeeded in turning your head."

"Bloody right. A waste of a man's energies, the creatures are."

"Oh, yes. Frivolous, the lot of them. You are better off avoiding them altogether, even if they possess the faces of angels."

"Just so," Darcy agreed. "It would not matter to me if the handsomest woman in all England were to alight just before me with a mind like a law student and the integrity of a saint."

"Naturally," Richard agreed. He carefully sniffed the length of his cigar, his expression detached and cool. "You would not even blink twice."

"Nor would I be troubled if such a person could nurse a poor opinion of me, just as Anne does. It is not for me to fret over each time my words and deeds have been misunderstood or I was judged to be arrogant for acting upon my own sound instincts."

"Certainly not. You need not defend yourself."

"No, indeed." Darcy nodded with a tip of his glass and a facetious half-smirk. "It would not matter if unicorns and faeries did exist in Derbyshire, for it is not as if I could take her for my bride."

"A pity about her lack of pedigree and fortune," Richard sympathised round the butt of the cigar.

"Those I could nearly overlook, if it were not…" Darcy bit off the last words and glared at his cousin. "But no such person exists."

"A pity, for I almost had you tricked into giving up her name!" Richard laughed. "Very well, there are no mythical beings in Derbyshire. But did I hear—it was probably only rumour—that you managed to marry off old Bernard Wickham before he died? That must have been satisfying, putting the nail in the coffin of George Wickham's aspirations, so to speak. I suppose I ought to congratulate you for bringing Bernard round to reason at last. Whom did you find to marry him?"

A sudden queasiness made Darcy's stomach clench and his face turn sour. "No one special. A reduced gentlewoman whose father's estate fell to the next male relative. You know the sort—there are dozens or perhaps hundreds of such women."

"Of course," Richard echoed as he stuck the cigar back between his teeth. "Nothing unique about such a woman at all."

Darcy met his cousin's eyes and discovered an odd twinkle there—a peculiar cunning that hearkened back to long-ago days of youth when one would discover the other's secret. But this time, the confession was too dear, too impossible. And so, he swallowed the last of his drink and rose to his feet.

"It was good to see you, Richard," he said. "Please give Anne my regards, and my hope that we may all meet under the same roof again as family."

Richard came to stand beside him and gave him his hand. "It was no punishment to see you either, old boy."

They walked together to the door, and Darcy stopped to offer a final expression of goodwill. "Will you come to Matlock this autumn? If you do, I hope you will come to Pemberley for a bit of shooting."

"Oh, I do not dare," Richard answered with a strange smile. "I hear the forests around Pemberley have unicorns."

E LIZABETH FOUND AN EXCUSE to remain at Pemberley that first Sunday after Mr Darcy's departure. Miss Darcy seemed depressed, she assured herself. She had her duties—now even more than before, for had it not been for her, the master of Pemberley would have remained at home and his sister would still be in comforts. Throughout the day when she would normally have gone to her family, she clung close by her charge, soothing herself that in this, at least, she was doing something right.

Whether Georgiana Darcy perceived the reason for Elizabeth's sombre manner could not be certain. However, on the following Sunday when Elizabeth proclaimed her intent to remain again, Georgiana would not hear of it. And so, to Corbett she went. The Bennet family attended church services together, then retired for an afternoon of leisure. Elizabeth and Jane pardoned themselves for a quiet ramble up the lane, having little to say and no particular object in mind.

Jane sighed nostalgically, gazing over the neighbouring field. "I am coming to like it here in Derbyshire very much, but it is still not quite like home. Do you remember how we all used to walk to Meryton of an afternoon?"

"Or to Lucas Lodge to see Charlotte," Elizabeth replied with a smile.

Jane's brow creased. "Better not recall her name in front of Mama. She still resents that Charlotte is now the mistress at Longbourn. Unjust, she calls it, saying the house should never have gone to Mr Collins."

"Poor Mama!" Elizabeth agreed.

"Oh, but she is growing more settled each day. That is all thanks to you, Lizzy. I know you still regret..."

"Regret?" Elizabeth crossed her arms and watched her feet as they walked. "That is not precisely right—at least, not as it was."

"No? That sounds like a different opinion than you professed before."

"Perhaps I learned something I did not know before."

Jane looked sceptically to her sister's face, but allowed the subject to rest when Elizabeth said no more. "Did you get the letter from Uncle Philips?"

"Yes. He said it was perfectly legal for me to sell Corbett Lodge to anyone I chose for any amount I deemed satisfactory, even as little as a pound. He also said there would be no impediment even if I wished to sell it to Mama or to you, since Mama is a widow and you are unmarried—no husband to claim it."

"I know." Jane laughed quietly. "Lydia opened it before I caught her. She tried to make the seal look as if she had not broken it, but when she was discovered she pulled it out again and read it to everyone."

"She is becoming sly! And brazen. We must guard her more carefully, I see."

"It is true, but I am more concerned just now with your notion of selling to one of us. Why would you do such a thing? Is it not enough that the house belongs to you?"

Elizabeth tightened her arms about her middle and lifted her shoulders. "I no longer feel that it was unjust that George Wickham did not receive his brother's property, but I am not yet comfortable calling it my own. Perhaps if I sold it to Mama, she would not suffer in her conscience as I do. It would either be her or you."

"You cannot think of it! You are the only one with the boldness to make the best of it. I... would not even want it."

Elizabeth smiled warmly at her sister. "Of course! I hope that soon you shall have no need of a house. You will be far more agreeably situated."

Jane blushed. "Mr Bingley has no serious designs, Lizzy. I shall not make myself unhappy over him."

"Ah, you say this, but you have already done so! Fear not, for I am sure the gentleman will return this autumn and you will see much of him then."

"Oh, do not embarrass me! Pray, let me defer thinking and speaking of him until I see that he truly has come back."

"If you wish."

"But Lizzy—" Jane stopped and turned seriously to her sister. "Truly, what is this business about transferring the ownership of Corbett to one of us? You are not considering it seriously, I hope."

Elizabeth frowned. "No. The idea was upon the recommendation of one I thought to trust, but now I see that perhaps it was little more than a diversion. I suppose if I ever entertained a suitor and desired that Corbett should remain a home for our mother and sisters, I could consider it again... but I expect one marriage was enough for me. Besides—" she offered Jane a wan smile—"it is not as if I have had gentlemen beating at the door. I shall remain forever as I am and be grateful."

"Dearest Lizzy! Do not give over the notion of your own happiness so easily. Somewhere, there is a gentleman who would count it an honour to win your regard." She impulsively embraced her sister, and with arms laced about each other's waists, they began walking again, each lost in her own thoughts. Some minutes later, they both stopped when another figure appeared in the road. "Lizzy, who is that woman?"

The woman appeared to be a farmer's wife, and when she saw them, she hastened her steps with apparent intent to speak to them. "I have never seen her," Elizabeth admitted.

The woman was not tall but walked with brisk purpose. She was carrying a basket that appeared to be too heavy for her, and when she drew near, it was difficult to judge her age. "Mrs Wickham?" she asked and dropped an immediate curtsey.

Elizabeth nodded. "I am. And you are?"

"Oh! Sakes, ma'am, I meant no disrespect. I'm Mrs Brown, and I were going to see a poor sick lad a quart' mile up the road. I tho' when I saw you tha' you must be the Mrs Wickham I've 'eard so much on."

"Indeed so. Why, in that case, I have been wishing to meet you as well. What is this you say about a sick lad?" Elizabeth asked.

"Jacob's boy," Mrs Brown answered. "Took sick last week. 'Tisn't serious, no' if I can get me draught to 'im."

"Are you a sort of apothecary?" Jane asked in wonder.

Mrs Brown shook her head. "Me da' was. I'm nought but a widow wha' knows a few remedies. I cure where I can for a few eggs or a bi' o' cheese, and sometimes nothin'."

"That is very fine," Elizabeth praised her. "I had heard nothing of you, other than you were a kind neighbour and were responsible for the rum cake my mother so fancied."

"'Tweren't nothin'," Mrs Brown answered. "I do wha' I can, since the landlord cares nothing for his folk. A brutish lord and master, he is."

Jane put her fingers to her lips. "Dreadful! I hope I do not know this landlord."

"I daresay you do," Mrs Brown replied solemnly. "Everyone for fifty miles knows Mr Darcy. But what is there to be done against such a man?"

Elizabeth was slitting her eyes and pursing her lips. "Indeed," was her careful response. "Have you had many dealings with Mr Darcy?"

"A great many. As I understand you have as well, Mrs Wickham, I would advise you not to trust everything you hear."

Jane gasped and turned pale at this ill report of a man of whom she had been inclined to think well, but Elizabeth only looked grave. "I will remember your cautions. As you are on a mission of mercy, I shall not keep you. It was a pleasure, Mrs Brown."

She inclined her head to the woman, then clasped Jane's hand to turn back the other way. "Jane," she whispered when the woman was safely behind them, "did you notice anything odd about the way she spoke?"

Jane glanced over her shoulder. "No. She talked just like all the other farmers."

"But that is just it!" Elizabeth hissed. "She spoke thus until she began slighting Mr Darcy. Then she was suddenly able to pronounce her 'h's and her inflections sounded more polished."

"Oh, Lizzy! You do sound far too suspicious. One would almost think you were searching for some conspiracy!"

"Perhaps I am. Mr Wickham spoke warmly of her, and I have since discovered reason to doubt his assertions. I think I shall ask Miss Darcy if she knows Mrs Brown."

Jane sighed and shook her head. "All I wanted was a pleasant walk this afternoon."

Elizabeth linked her arm through her sister's. "Dearest Jane! Let us go on, then, and have no more talk of Wickhams or Darcys or anything but that which gives us pleasure."

Strangely, however, Mr Darcy was foremost in her thoughts all the rest of the day.

Twelve

September 1812

D ARCY NUDGED HIS MOUNT into an elegant trot, taking some satisfaction in the way the mare arched her glossy neck and lifted each step with elastic suspension. The creature had been worth every penny of the exorbitant price demanded by Viscount Atterbury, for she never failed to turn heads in Hyde Park. Not that turning heads was ever his ambition, of course. But, occasionally, it was convenient, such as when a man's mind was turning numb from boredom and he was in the mood for a brief conversation with no threat of anything more demanding.

"Darcy!" A hand raised in the carriage he approached, and Darcy drew up.

"Lord Matlock," Darcy greeted his uncle, then tipped his hat to the ladies in his carriage. "Lady Matlock and Lady Sophia. A pleasure to see you this afternoon."

"Likewise," Matlock answered. "Richard was by last week, and he said you paid him a call. Why have we not seen more of you?"

"I must beg your pardon. I have been much occupied, I am afraid."

The earl grunted. "Let that not stop you. You must come to dinner on Tuesday. No, no, I absolutely insist. Lady Matlock has been longing to host you again."

Darcy considered the notion. He had always enjoyed the company of his Fitzwilliam relations, and he truly did need to begin conversing with Lady Matlock about Georgiana's come-out. It might be just the thing. But then he permitted his gaze to rove to Lady Sophia and the cold, almost assured look in her eye, and a chill rippled down his spine.

"I am afraid I have another obligation," he answered politely. "But perhaps we might go to White's together."

"Of course, Darcy. Yes, that would be most agreeable."

Darcy touched the butt of his whip to his hat once more. "Tuesday next, then. Good afternoon, Lord Matlock, Lady Matlock."

"Good afternoon, Darcy. I—no, hold a moment! I had nearly forgot why I wished to see you." The earl turned to his driver and his wife, making his excuses, then, shockingly, stepped down from his carriage. "A word, if you please."

Darcy tried to conceal his astonishment, following Lord Matlock to the side of the path. "Is there some urgent concern, my lord?"

"A rumour, and it concerns you. You were the one managing Bernard Wickham's affairs, were you not?"

"I was. He had many 'affairs' requiring management."

"I imagine he did, the wastrel, but there may yet be one more. Were you aware of a legal complaint regarding his parentage?"

Darcy narrowed his eyes. "Who makes such an accusation?"

"I do not yet know. I only heard this from a private investigator your father and I once employed, who came to warn me of the matter. I rewarded his loyalty handsomely, of course, and asked to be kept apprised. Shall I send you word when more is known?"

Darcy's fist tightened on the reins. "Please do."

"Lizzy! Would you just look what Mr Wickham has brought?"

It was late one Sunday afternoon, and Elizabeth had decided to attend services with Georgiana before joining her own sisters. Lydia's question shook her badly, and she hung up her bonnet then turned round in some astonishment. "What?"

"Oh, come! You will not believe it." Lydia caught Elizabeth's elbow and dragged her reluctant sister into the dining room, where her mother and other sisters had gathered round the table gazing raptly at a whole roast leg of lamb. And at the head of the table, looking like some benevolent patron, stood George Wickham.

"Greetings, Sister." He came to her side, bowing with a flourish and offering his most charming smile. "I was not certain you would be joining us, as I understand you have not come every Sunday of late. I do hope there is no trouble at Pemberley."

Elizabeth kept her expression carefully neutral as she laid aside her wrap. "None whatsoever. May I ask to what we owe the pleasure of such a feast, sir?"

"Oh! A bit of nothing this is. A friendly wager with a well-to-do farmer, and I found myself the owner of this magnificent roast. I asked myself, 'What shall I do with all this?' and the answer was clear as day. But, my dear sister, you do not seem pleased. I hope I have not caused offense by my offering."

She forced a smile and a gentle shake of her head. "Of course not."

"Excellent," said he, "for I have not yet done." He placed his hand behind his back, pausing theatrically and waiting for her eyes to fix on his face. "Voila!" he cried and presented her with a small box.

Elizabeth hesitated, not accepting it at once, and his expression altered from buoyant to wounded. "I hope I have not troubled you, Elizabeth. Is a brother-in-law not permitted to give his sister-in-law a gift?"

"I am not certain it is seemly," she confessed. "What would people say?"

"I hope they will say that George Wickham is a generous fellow who cares prodigiously for anyone who can claim a connection to him. Your good mother did not object."

"My mother?" Elizabeth turned to find Mrs Bennet in the very act of touching a small jet brooch, pinned to her gown. "You gave my mother a brooch?"

"And a modest amber cross for each of your sisters, as well—I did not think it quite the thing to give unmarried ladies a brooch. I hope you will forgive me. Come, you must look at it! All the finest ladies prize jet jewellery while in mourning, yet its costliness might have prevented my favourite ladies from wearing such pieces in memory of their father and husband. I sought to remedy that."

Elizabeth thinned her lips and opened the box. Inside was a tiny flower pin, black as night and glittering from its linen nest. "I thank you, Mr Wickham, but I cannot accept."

"What is this, 'Mr Wickham'? Have you grown formal with me, my dear sister?"

She closed the lid of the box and tried, in vain, to give it back. "No, but I must be conscious of appearances."

Wickham's countenance darkened. "This is not about accepting gifts, is it? You are more concerned about Darcy's opinion."

"Should I not be? My duties are as a guide and chaperon to his sister, and I am most often in his house. Does not my employer have a right to an opinion regarding my affairs?"

"Not if those personal affairs do not affect him. How can a simple brooch be of concern? I hope—" he touched his hand to her forearm and leaned close—close enough to send a shiver down her spine. "I hope you have not heeded Darcy in all things. He has only his own interests at heart."

Elizabeth glanced down at Mr Wickham's hand and coolly stepped back until he dropped it. "Please, sir, pay me the honour of regarding my wishes in this. I speak not for Mr Darcy's sake, but my own. You are very generous, but it would be better if you did not continue bringing gifts."

He frowned. "As you say, Elizabeth. I hope I am not unwelcome here."

"Unwelcome?" Mrs Bennet had been speaking to Kitty, but she overheard Mr Wickham's remarks at a most inopportune moment and came near to speak her mind. "Why could you think yourself unwelcome, Mr Wickham? Lizzy, whatever have you said to poor Mr Wickham?"

"A misunderstanding, Mrs Bennet," Mr Wickham quickly interrupted. "Nothing to worry about. Our dear Elizabeth is only expressing her very sound reservations regarding the acceptance of gifts from a single gentleman. A wise lady—" he bowed graciously, "and I humbly submit to her wishes."

"Nonsense, Lizzy!" Mrs Bennet scoffed. "Why, it is not as if Mr Wickham has singled you out inappropriately, but he has showered us all with his kindness. Is that not right, Mr Wickham?"

He inclined his head. "As you say, but I would not wish to cause any discomfort or ill feelings."

"Do not be ridiculous! Come, the table is laid. Lizzy, take that dirty wrap out from the dining room."

Elizabeth surrendered, though Jane gave her a curious look as she passed by. Chastened, Elizabeth schooled her expression to be as neutral as she could make it and determined to avoid making a scene.

"WHAT A SCENE! JANE, I cannot recall when I have been more humiliated!"

Elizabeth slammed the door to Jane's bedroom and sank forcefully onto the creaking bed. "How does she dare?"

"Lydia can be too outspoken," Jane agreed, "but it was not so bad."

"Not so bad! She fairly bragged to Mr Wickham that I meant to deed Corbett Lodge to her when I remarried—and my supposed lover! Jane, what could make Lydia suppose that there was anything between Mr Darcy and me?"

"Do you mean there is nothing?" Jane asked innocently.

Elizabeth dropped the hand that had been kneading her brow. "Of course not! Are you saying that you also thought—"

Jane shrugged. "I think everyone does. It is true, I have only met him a few times, but each time he entered a room, he looked first for you before going to anyone else."

"Because I am employed at his house!"

"And there is his tone of voice and expression when he speaks to you."

"Again," Elizabeth huffed, "he is familiar with my presence and I do not require him to engage in small-talk—"

"Confess it, Lizzy! You find him attractive as well. Come, now, I have seen how you watch him when he is looking away."

"How could I not? The man is infuriating!"

"Is that why you stare at him? And my goodness, how you needle him! You have not bickered so energetically with anyone since Papa. A stranger would think you to be fighting in anger, but I believe you both take much pleasure from such exchanges."

"You mistake me, Jane. I owe Mr Darcy my respect, that is all. If I relate to him differently than others, is it not to be expected? I am in his house all week, and he is entirely responsible for our family's comfort. Should I not spare him some civility?"

"But what does he owe you? Certainly, far less than he has already given. Confess it, Lizzy—there is something, is there not?"

"I... no, Jane. Perhaps we have a peculiar way of getting on, but all this means nothing. Men of Mr Darcy's station do not take notice of their younger sisters' companions."

Jane tilted her head and raised her brows. "Then why are you blushing?"

Elizabeth quickly pressed her palms to her cheeks. "I am not. But we are not speaking of me. What are we to do with Lydia?"

Jane shrugged. "She is only fifteen. What girl of her age does not speak some embarrassment or other? I am sure Mr Wickham will be generous and refrain from repeating anything she said."

Elizabeth rolled her eyes. "Perhaps Mr Wickham is one of the principle people I would not wish to hear Lydia's folly."

"Surely it is nothing. I think you are weary, Lizzy, and you are fretting more than you need to. Has Mr Darcy sent word of his London business? I do hope he returns soon to ease Miss Darcy and relieve some of your worries."

"I would not count on seeing Mr Darcy again soon," Elizabeth muttered. "And perhaps it is for the best."

L ADY SOPHIA WAS NO longer wearing mourning black when Darcy called at the Earl of Matlock's London house the following week. He glanced at his cousin a second time in some surprise. Richard had not exaggerated when he claimed his sister would be seeking another husband soon, for the lady had donned a highly... diverting gown. She even appeared to be painted—or as close to such a scandalous state as an earl's daughter would dare tread during the morning hours.

"Lady Matlock, Lady Sophia." He bowed to both his aunt and cousin at the drawing room before the footman announced that his uncle would see him in the study. He gave his promise to both ladies that he would not depart without taking tea.

The earl rose from his desk to greet him warmly, and with very little preamble. "Ah, Darcy, I am glad you came when you did. This came not an hour ago—what do you make of it?" He extended a note. "It looks to me as if someone thinks to discredit your father in his grave. Bloody indecent!"

Darcy's brow furrowed as he read the tightly penned lines—the words "foundling" and "forgery" leaping out more than once. "What is this?" he asked. "A claim that Bernard was not legally acknowledged by Franklin Wickham during his lifetime? Preposterous. Everyone can attest to the fact that the senior Wickham considered Bernard his son and heir. It cannot be contested—there can be no grounds for this complaint."

The earl cleared his throat. "The fact that a mere steward could call his son an 'heir' to anything does raise the question, I suppose. But I cannot see how anyone could succeed legally with such an argument."

"Perhaps that is not the complainant's objective. Blackening my family's name would do."

The earl's features hardened. "I think you know where to start looking for this trou-blemaker. See it hushed up, Darcy."

Darcy gestured with the note. "I will keep this, if you do not object."

"By all means. I trust I will hear no more of the matter."

Darcy took tea with his aunt and cousin, although the earl declined to join them. Lady Matlock employed the time fretting about Richard and his scandalously small flat—after all, as a married man, he ought to have given it up in search of a better situation. Lady Sophia heartily added her sentiments that the marital estate ought to increase wealth at each essay, and that a married man who still sought to live economically was nothing short of a disgrace.

Darcy merely sipped his tea and kept his own counsel.

Thirteen

"Mrs Brown, you called the lady?" Georgiana Darcy dropped heavily on the sofa and looked blankly at the wall. "No, I do not know her. You met her?"

"Twice now. The first time, I thought her manners were peculiar but not alarming. Today, she claimed to happen upon me 'accidentally,' but no one ever takes that path unless they know it is a favourite of mine. I suspected that someone told her where I might be found and that she means to ingratiate herself to me."

"And you said she knew Mr Wickham?"

"I do not like to distress you by asking such a question," Elizabeth said as she sat by the girl's side. "I understand you are not… not friends with Mr Wickham, but I am becoming concerned and you are the only one I can ask. When I first met George Wickham, he recommended two ladies to my notice. One was the Mrs Godfrey we met in Lambton, and I am already suspicious of her."

"So was William," Georgiana interjected.

"Yes, he said that," Elizabeth confessed. "What troubles me is the other lady commended by Mr Wickham was this Mrs Brown. I wonder what your brother would have to say about her."

"What did she look like?"

"Short in stature, green eyes and fair hair. A face that looks mature but lacks any lines of age. And she had a small mole on her left cheek."

Georgiana shivered and reached for Elizabeth's hand. "That sounds like her—yes, it does! Mrs Younge, I mean, my old companion. But why would it be she?"

"She must have been friends with George Wickham. I believe it would not be inappropriate this time to fancy what you may, after the fashion of your novels. But if it is true, and it is she, I wonder what reason Mr Wickham had for recommending two such women to me as companions. What could he be seeking?"

Georgiana's mouth turned down in a severe pout, almost a scowl. "Money. That is all he ever wants, and he thinks you have what should be his. You do not think he would mean to trouble you or your sisters, do you?"

Elizabeth pursed her lips and blinked. "I wish I knew."

"William will know," Georgiana assured her friend. "I shall write to him at once."

"Oh, please do not!" Elizabeth protested, but before the words had died from her lips, she understood their futility. Mr Darcy must be told of her suspicions—to fail to do so would be an abdication of her post and a betrayal of the trust he had placed in her. "That is," she added slowly, "perhaps... perhaps I ought to write to him."

"Why you?"

"Because..." Elizabeth felt her chest tighten and forced herself to take a steady breath. "Because if you wrote to him, he would be concerned about your security and peace of mind. That would be inappropriate in this case, would it not?"

"But how are your concerns not my own?" Georgiana objected. "William has always taken an interest in the troubles of others, so why should I not?"

"You forget—" Elizabeth smiled affectionately—"I am hardly without a voice of my own, as I have found occasionally to my regret."

Dear Sir,

If you have broken the seal of this letter and learned who writes to you without casting the pages into the flames, I congratulate you on your forbearance.

Be assured that Miss Darcy is in good spirits and I have done nothing terribly shocking, save for taking up my pen to write to an unmarried man. Though you know my character well enough to understand that I delight in absurdity and am by no means a suitable counsellor for an impressionable young lady, my purpose in writing to you was neither to offend nor to astonish. However, I am not writing in a professional capacity, which might have been seemly.

I seek your advice on a matter of personal concern, and as you have relayed pertinent information by means of a letter, I shall do the same. Recently, I made the acquaintance of one Mrs Brown, who represented herself to be a farmer's widow. She was not remarkable in herself, but for some oddities in her manner and the defamatory way in which she spoke of a certain landowner.

This alone should not give pause, for I know quite well that this self-same landowner is a perturbing fellow with a terribly aggravating habit of provoking me to words I frequently regret afterward. No one could feel anything but sympathy for another woman similarly burdened by proximity to this nettlesome individual, but for the fact that Mrs Brown's acquaintance had been recommended to me by the calumnious lips of one I am obliged to call my lawful brother.

Perhaps it is illogical—indeed, most probably indicative of a suspicious and unbalanced mind—but the association made me uneasy. I hope you will now do your proper duty and terminate my employment when I confess that yesterday I took my qualms directly to Miss Darcy, even while knowing that speaking a particular gentleman's name would rightly unsettle her. I fear the ensuing conversation did nothing to comfort either of us, for neither she nor any of your servants had ever heard of the good and virtuous "Mrs Brown" of a certain miscreant's fabrication.

Before you conclude—possibly rightly—that I have cast my reason out with my dignity and am now little more than a flighty widow who forever clutches at her lace and trembles at the slightest hint of intrigue, I pray you recall that you are not the only being in possession of a younger sister. As mine are tripled in number and yet have considerably less discretion than yours, I must be even more vigilant in their associations. When I received a note from my eldest sister not half an hour ago that this well-known rascal made a social call on my family with yet another rum cake, courtesy of this Mrs Brown, I settled it with myself that my discomfort over the matter exceeded my reluctance to write a letter to a gentleman. It is my first such transgression of modesty—what do you think of my effort? Have I sufficiently breeched the bounds of all that is polite and demure?

I shall await your appropriately outraged reply. Shall you desire me to pour ashes over my head and go on bare feet when you demand my removal from your house? Pray, spare me no portion of your just umbrage for my audacity in all these matters, for I shall now pen yet one final, and most shocking (I suppose I did intend to astonish and offend, after all) confession. I find it most entertaining when you are vexed. Surely, that is all the evidence necessary that mine is a thoroughly irreverent character.

I do, however, ask that with your response, you would include some advice. If I have learnt one thing of your character, it is that you always know, or at least appear to know, what is to be done.

Not in the least yours,

EW

D ARCY'S VERY EARS WERE warm when he re-read the letter. Again.

The impertinent tart. Any other man would sack her. It... was an intriguing notion.

He felt a smile tugging at his lips even as his mind began to spin on her suppositions. She would never have written unless at the end of need, and most particularly would never have asked Georgiana's thoughts on the matter without some deep suspicion troubling her. How it must have stung her pride to ask his advice!

He was at the door of his study before he had even pulled his coat back on. "Parker, tell Mrs Dobbs I will be departing for Derbyshire in the morning, and send word to the coachman as well."

The footman bowed his "Yes, sir," and raced to do the master's bidding. Darcy turned back to his desk, agitated and, oddly, indecisive. Why was he mounting a fast coach back to Derbyshire at the whimsy and insecurity of a mere companion, a woman of hardly any account whatsoever?

The answer rang clearly in his heart, and with it, an equal tremor of regret in his spirit. Because the woman was Elizabeth, that was why.

"G O TO PEMBERLEY WITH you? Whatever for?" Richard cocked his frame back in his chair and made a face at Darcy. "I thought I was not even welcome there."

"Of course, you are. As you shall always be. I had hoped to mend this breach in our fellowship, and Georgiana has missed you."

"But you speak of going tomorrow! Even if I understood the haste, I could not. Anne is here, did you not know? She arrived yesterday and is in high dudgeon that she missed seeing you so she might have the pleasure of scolding you all over again. I daren't go to

Pemberley without at least inviting her, for if I do, I will bring upon myself the wrath of both my wife and my mother-in-law. It is a fate more brutal than Boney's cannon."

"Then Anne must come as well. Perhaps she might finally exhaust her grievances about me and be content."

"I cannot merely bring Anne! She and my sister are thick as thieves. I will hear nothing the entire journey but that she has no one to speak to and none to sympathise with her odious plight." This last, Richard pronounced in a heavily inflected tone.

"Then bring Lady Sophia as well, if it gives Anne pleasure—heaven knows I must be in want of feminine oversight, and between the two of them I ought to be well supplied."

Richard narrowed his eyes. "Both of them? You cannot be serious. What are you about, Darcy?"

"You look for mystery when there is none. I need a man of your powers, and time is likely of the essence."

"Of all the…" Richard muttered to himself as he thought, then his countenance brightened in inspiration. "Wickham. Do you need a man to run him through? I would consider it a privilege!"

"That shall not be necessary, but you do know how delicate the matter is." Darcy sealed his mouth then and waited, observing his cousin's wary manner.

"I know what you will say next if I do not agree. You will be certain to inform me that it is in my best interest to come, my wife will be better pleased, Lady Catherine will not be likely to follow all the way to Derbyshire, etcetera."

"Naturally," Darcy said with a nonchalant wave. "I do not consider only myself."

Richard nodded slowly. "I will come, so long as I may bring my sword."

"Elizabeth, look!" Georgiana Darcy dropped her needlework and rushed to the nearest window. "It is Fitzwilliam!" she cried.

Elizabeth came more slowly, her steps weighted by no small measure of dread even as a great cloud of doubt lifted from her thoughts. "He has come sooner even than I expected," she murmured.

"That is Fitzwilliam's way. He would not send a letter to tell us of his arrival when he could come as quickly himself. My goodness, look how lathered the horses are!"

They watched together as the team drew to a halt in the drive and a coachman stepped quickly to the door. Then a figure emerged—a long arm, a broad shoulder, an exquisitely meticulous mess of dark curls covered immediately by a grey beaver, and, at last, a face that looked curiously to the window where they stood.

Mr Darcy.

He offered the briefest of smiles, but though Georgiana bounced in pleasure at his recognition, Elizabeth sensed his eyes locking on herself. His expression sobered and lingered... one pulse... two... then Elizabeth felt nearly chilled when he broke the look and turned back to the carriage.

She released a slow, shaken breath. Since when did the sensation of Mr Darcy looking at her make her flush like a schoolgirl? It must surely be her embarrassment over the past, and a just measure of humility due to the present.

But then, another feeling struck her, this one with all the force of lead and the searing pain of fire. Mr Darcy was handing a fine creature down from the carriage behind him—one who beamed and smiled and clung to his arm while she gazed adoringly up at him.

"Cousin Sophia!" Georgiana gasped in pleasure. "And Richard! Oh, and Cousin Anne! Come, Elizabeth, you must meet them!" She dashed away, pausing only at the door to compose herself before entering the main hall.

Elizabeth followed, a vast deal more slowly. She was in the entry, standing at Georgiana's shoulder as she ought when the party came up the steps, but she managed to successfully avoid his eyes.

Much to her later dismay, it had not been difficult. Mr Darcy had looked at no one but his sister and his guests. Even at the obligatory introductions, he only gestured casually at her while uttering her name as nonchalantly as that of the common servants. His attention was immediately redirected to the ladies, for one of them—the colonel's wife—began to protest her fatigue and general malaise, fairly commanding her host to secure her a hot bath and private quarters.

Elizabeth drew her lip between her teeth and unconsciously shrank back. The colonel's sister, Lady Sophia, was alternating between petting Georgiana, crooning over Anne Fitzwilliam, and unnecessarily soothing the ever-unruffled Mr Darcy.

Only Colonel Fitzwilliam caught her eye, and it was with a peculiar interest that caused her to shiver. He tilted his head slightly and his lip twitched, as if he had confirmed some notion to himself. But then, he had not the decency to look away and leave her to her discomfort—no; he bowed and gestured for her to precede him up the stairs behind Georgiana.

The hair stood on the back of her neck all the way up the steps. He was studying her—she sensed it by the way his steps sounded evenly in time with hers and even faint hesitations on her part caused him to halt altogether. It was a sick and heavy feeling, being invisible and conspicuous all at once, but such she was—the fallen gentlewoman, no doubt an object of derision among the noble Fitzwilliams, and perhaps even a figure of intrigue to a man safely married elsewhere.

At her earliest opportunity, she moved towards Georgiana. "Miss Darcy, if you do not require my presence for the next half hour, I should like to retire."

Georgiana blinked. "Of course, Elizabeth. Are you well? I thought you would wish to speak with Fitzwilliam at once."

Elizabeth tipped her head across the hall where the gentleman himself was speaking quietly to Lady Sophia. "Later, perhaps, if Mr Darcy is not otherwise occupied. I prefer to rest my head for now."

The girl's brow furrowed, but she agreed. "I will have Mrs Reynolds send up some peppermint. Oh, it is so very good though, is it not? Having Fitzwilliam back, I mean. We shall be so merry, and now you needn't worry about anything!"

Elizabeth offered a thin smile. "Nothing at all."

Fourteen

M RS WICKHAM DID NOT come down until dinner, and when she did arrive, she slipped wordlessly to Georgiana's side and seemed to take no notice of him.

Darcy was careful not to make her uncomfortable by looking her way across the table—unless, of course, he sensed that her attention was elsewhere. Those few glances he did snatch were telling. She wore a non-descript, mouse-grey gown—not unsuited to her half-mourning, but entirely inappropriate for her complexion and figure. She must have resumed styling her hair herself, because he could not imagine any lady's maid in his employ fashioning such a plain, dowdy coiffure when the lady had such lustrous, thick hair to work with. And her colour... was she feverish or blushing?

"Oh, Mr Darcy, I pray, do tell me what you think."

He drew a short breath and commanded his senses once more before turning to Lady Sophia, seated beside him. "I beg your pardon?"

"Why, what we were just talking of! Mother was speaking of plans for Georgiana's come-out, and she sought my opinion on her gowns. After all, Mother has no patience for sitting through hours upon hours of fittings any longer. I cannot think how wearisome she finds it all, for you know how her back pains her these days. Anyway, she had already selected some shades and fabrics for Georgiana, but I told her—you must think me dreadfully irreverent—I said they were all rubbish, and we must begin all over with bolder shades and heavier silk. Am I not right? A girl of her station must stand out, should she not?"

"There are many ways in which a young lady may 'stand out,' as you put it. She needn't attire herself as a peacock just to turn the eye."

"Ah, Mr Darcy, you speak like an older brother, but you must think like a single gentleman. She must first catch the eye, before aught else, for who knows but that the most eligible gentleman may find his attention diverted by another female with brighter plumage? And by then, all hope is lost, do you see?"

"If he is so easily diverted with no head to look for more than bright feathers, then I daresay he is not the man I desire for my future brother."

Lady Sophia laughed. "Mother said you would think thus, but no matter. We shall have Georgiana turned out as a princess when the time comes, and you will hardly know her when she enters the room. Is that not right, Anne? You have heard our plans, and can you say you do not approve?"

Anne cast a casual eye over Georgiana, who was shrinking in her chair, and gave a careless flip of her hand. "Naturally, she ought to appear in a fashion worthy of her station, but I think it hardly matters. Georgiana Darcy would hardly need to show her face at all, and she could command the best suitors. With a fortune such as hers, success is practically guaranteed, so long as she does not waste her youth and looks in waiting on the indecisive sort." She blinked slowly and bestowed a long, cold look on Darcy before drawing a sip of her champagne.

Darcy felt an uncomfortable burn forming along the ridges of his ears, but he made a show of not hearing Anne's pointed jab. Richard, however, was less tactful. His cousin muttered something incoherent, then tossed his napkin over his plate and rose. He made a curt bow to Mrs Wickham, who was seated near him, then he left the room without another word to anyone else.

"Ah, dear Richard," sighed Lady Sophia. "Mother is forever speaking to him about his temper. What can have set him off this time?"

No one bothered to answer, and the rest of the meal was carried on in near silence.

ELIZABETH PERFORMED HER DUTY by Miss Darcy that evening—sitting near her at dinner and giving reassuring glances whenever certain topics made her uneasy. Later, she turned pages for her at the pianoforte when the family's appeals induced the shy girl to play for the party. Colonel Fitzwilliam never returned, which Elizabeth found odd. No one else seemed to miss him, which she found even odder.

Mr Darcy was nearly silent all evening. He sat in a long chair by the window, occasionally gazing at it as though he could see into the blackness of the night. When he was not looking there, his eyes seemed to rest upon his cousins with a peculiar gleam. Elizabeth had not been so many months in his house without recognising something of that expression. Mr Darcy seldom spared a thought for those persons who were unremarkable, which meant that he found something either appealing or abhorrent in the ladies. Given the gentle replies he made whenever they spoke directly to him, Elizabeth decided it was the former case.

"Elizabeth?" Georgiana whispered. "I do not recall the next bit."

Elizabeth looked at the music page and realised that she had lost track of Georgiana's playing. Talented musician that she was, she had continued from memory for as long as she could, but now the piano had gone quiet and all eyes had turned to them. She managed a flustered apology and turned two entire pages over to catch up to the place where Georgiana had left off.

"Something the matter, darling?" Lady Sophia asked. "Why, the poor child is grown weary. Anne, my dear, we have been unkind to our young cousin, asking her to keep us entertained all evening."

"I do not see how she can be fatigued after a mere hour," Mrs Fitzwilliam replied. "Darcy always assured Mama that Georgiana played 'very constantly.' Is that not right, Darcy? I wonder if it can be true, as you claim."

Georgiana was quietly gathering her music, looking down to avoid the gazes of any in the room, but Elizabeth was watching Mr Darcy. He had slanted his tall figure back in his chair, his head tipped in the manner of a man at leisure, and he offered a laconic frown to his cousin's query. "I am not in the habit of speaking untruths."

"But are all your claims valid?" asked the lady. "I daresay you have believed things that were not true."

"Such as?" he asked in what appeared to be mild interest.

"Truly, Darcy, such a thing would not be for me to say. However, if you were predisposed for or against a certain person, can you say that your judgment would never err?"

"I expect no one can say as much, though I have made it the study of my life to avoid such mistakes."

"And you would not leave a person in doubt about your opinions of them?" Mrs Fitzwilliam pressed, her tones brittle.

"Never, unless they were determined not to hear, or unless the confession of such an opinion would give pain."

The lady made a derisive expression to her companion. "I have never known you to be greatly troubled over the feelings of others, Darcy."

"Now, my dear Anne," Lady Sophia soothed, "did not Darcy think of your comfort when he invited me on this little visit to Pemberley? Goodness knows, it was not for my own sake."

"You do him too much credit, Sophia. I know very well what he is about, and my comfort had little to do with it."

Elizabeth discovered only belatedly that she was still watching Mr Darcy, for his eyes shifted in her direction when Georgiana discreetly excused herself from the piano bench. His gaze brushed lightly over his sister, settled on Elizabeth for a half a pulse beat, then flitted away, leaving her feeling both rumpled in spirit and superfluous to the moment. She quietly rose and could not decide whether she was dismayed or relieved that he gave her no further notice as she walked by him towards the door.

"On the contrary, Anne," he said in a cheerful tone, "your pleasure was chief among my concerns. Every host wishes for his guest—particularly if she be a lady—to have a close companion in the party in whom she might confide and take comfort."

Lady Sophia offered one of her cultured trills of laughter. "There, do you see, Anne? He pays us both a compliment."

"Or he means to insult us both," Anne Fitzwilliam retorted drily. "Darcy always means more than he says."

"I meant no insult," Mr Darcy answered. "But I do always speak the truth. I thought of my own pleasure as much as yours when arranging for your stay." He finished this remark with a warm smile at Lady Sophia, then turned his attention to his drink.

Elizabeth could bear no more. She had traversed the room slowly, finding an excuse to close the piano or gather Georgiana's forgotten shawl as she went, but now she turned away in humiliation. Whatever heedless words had once slipped from Mr Darcy's lips or flowed from his pen, it was clear that he had now thought better of them.

It was for the best. Truly—she had been right before when she had reminded him that any alliance between themselves would be reprehensible. And yet... there was that nagging thrill in her heart whenever he was close, a comfortable resonance whenever she looked upon his face, and a pleasant shiver up the back of her neck whenever his voice sounded in her ear. She had grown fond of being near him, accustomed to his sardonic witticisms, and rather enamoured of... well, that thought was better forgotten.

Elizabeth was now alone in the hall and quite put out with herself for having lost track of Miss Darcy. The young mistress was likely already upstairs dressing for bed, but Elizabeth could feel no sense of weariness or fatigue. Rather, she was restless, and craved a long, soothing book. She gave Miss Darcy's shawl to a maid and bent her steps towards the library.

She lingered some while, pondering over the selections more out of fretfulness than indecision. Nothing suited her tastes, but at last she settled on an old favourite, thinking that within its pages, at least, she would be at peace. Tucking it close to her chest, she turned around and nearly screamed when she discovered Colonel Fitzwilliam leaning against the stack just behind her. She fell back, covering her mouth and trying to compose herself.

"My apologies, Mrs Wickham. I did not intend to startle you."

She steadied her breath and amended her posture to something more dignified. "I protest that you must have intended to startle me, standing so close and approaching so silently as you did."

One side of his mouth tugged upwards and his blue eyes slowly roved from her head to her toes and back again. "Intriguing," he muttered under his breath. "I would offer to help you find something, but it appears you already have."

She glanced at the cover of her book, then repositioned it just before her chest. "Indeed. If you will excuse me, sir—"

"Pray, Mrs Wickham, a moment. I had been hoping to speak privately with you and now is an opportune time." He stepped nearer, his manner a curious mixture of masculine assertiveness and warmth.

Elizabeth drew back until she pressed against the shelf. "I will ask you to keep a respectable distance, sir."

The colonel stopped, one brow arched. "What is... oh! I see how it is. The lord of the manor routine, eh? You have nothing to fear from me, Mrs Wickham. Faith, I warrant that Darcy would skin me and place my head on a pike if I gave you any offence."

Elizabeth relaxed somewhat. "He might speak in my favour, but I doubt, sir, that Mr Darcy would take up my grievances against his own cousin with such vehemence as you claim."

The colonel gave another crooked smile and his eyes seemed to circle round Elizabeth's face once more. "Let us not test which of us is correct. What I meant to ask you, if I may, pertains to your esteemed brother-in-law. When was the last you saw him?"

Elizabeth blinked at this sudden shift from her expectations and tried to recall the facts. "A fortnight ago. My younger sister said on Sunday that he had gone to London just after his last call. If you wished to see him, perhaps you would have done better to remain where you were."

"Perhaps." The colonel crossed one leg over the other and leaned more heavily against the shelves. "What makes you think I came to see Wickham?"

"Why... the very fact that you asked me about him," Elizabeth stammered with some indignation.

The colonel scoffed. "If I need to speak with George Wickham, I have no trouble finding him. Nor do I need to ascertain with my own eyes that the cretin still draws breath, for I have sufficient contacts anywhere he might think to go."

"Then I do not understand why you would desire to speak with me about him. Perhaps you should address Mr Darcy to learn what you wish."

"No..." He pursed his lips and studied her face. "I have already learned a great deal. Have you spoken often with Mr Wickham?"

"Some. He appears to wish to be friendly with me, but after I understood... certain things about his character, I decided to remain more circumspect."

He laughed, but the humour did not touch his eyes. "Few are the women who hold to such a resolve when it is George Wickham working upon them. I know none who do not eventually fall to his charms."

Elizabeth lifted her chin and shifted the book in her arms to one side. "I submit to you that you do not know me, Colonel. Excuse me, please."

He stepped aside and allowed her to pass, but then turned after her. "Pray, Mrs Wickham, one more thing, if I may."

Elizabeth stopped and drew a long sigh before turning back. "Yes, Colonel?"

"My wife and my sister—what are your opinions on them?"

She glanced away and wetted her lips before answering. "I beg your pardon, Colonel, but I am merely employed here. I do not have the luxury of opinions."

"Aha, but you have formed them, nonetheless! I can see it in the way you clench your teeth whenever they speak."

"I think you are mistaken, Colonel. My one responsibility here is to be a friend and counsellor to Miss Darcy. It is a duty I take seriously, and one in which I am determined not to be found wanting—at least, not more so than I was already. If I should seem ill at ease, it is all due to concern for her, not myself."

The colonel nodded slowly. "You have a sharp tongue, Mrs Wickham. That alone does not recommend you to your current post."

"A fact that Mr Darcy must surely regret. I understand you perfectly, Colonel."

He raised his brows. "You do, do you? Hmm." He raised a finger to stroke his upper lip, then gave one more terse nod. "Well, Darcy must know what he is about. I imagine matters will change rather soon, and Georgiana will no longer have need of a companion."

She tilted her head. "Of what do you speak?"

"Why, when Darcy marries, of course. He has been reluctant coming to the point—some nonsense about trying to avoid marrying back into certain family connections—but his feelings and intentions would be obvious even to a blind man. We will have a wedding this winter, I wager."

Elizabeth turned away, her cheeks hot and her stomach crawling oddly. "Good evening, Colonel," she managed.

"Are you not taking the book you selected?" he called after her.

She glanced down and discovered that at some point in the colonel's revelation, she had pushed the precious book back on the shelf and now stood empty-handed. She looked at it longingly—if only it could settle her! "No," she decided. "I am no longer in the mood for reading. Good night."

Fifteen

"W HEN DID YOU SAY Bingley was coming back?" Colonel Fitzwilliam helped himself to a decanter of brandy from the sideboard and sauntered back to the billiards table.

"I did not say, but I expect him tomorrow. I was rather surprised he is not here already."

"And you believe he will offer for Mrs Wickham?"

Darcy twisted his cue, adjusting to the feel of it as he lined up his shot. "It would serve them both well if he did." He missed and stood back in mind frustration.

Fitzwilliam retrieved his own cue and studied the table. "She would suit him hand-somely. Better than fair features, seems to be a loyal sort of woman, and she has a bit of spine. But what say you, Darcy, how do you think of a couple where the wife is the more determined of the two? What chances have they for success and happiness?"

Darcy watched Richard drop his mark and considered. "Many men would take issue with a woman who is both clever and stubborn, as Mrs Wickham is. I think it nonsense, for a man would be fortunate to have such a stalwart partner in life. Bingley could do with a bit of direction, and is so easy in general that Mrs Wickham could hardly find anything in him to run against."

"Just so. But what of the lady's preferences? How do you think she would fare without a bit of flint upon which to sharpen her blade?"

Darcy smiled and made his next shot. "Even in retirement, you still speak as a soldier. You make Mrs Wickham out to be some she-devil, but I assure you, she is not."

"Aye, but mark my words; she will become dull within a twelve-month. A woman such as she likes a man who can go toe-to-toe and eye-to-eye with her. Now, if she married Bingley, I've no doubt that she would think herself well contented and have every reason for satisfaction—in the beginning. She may even grow fat, producing one chubby red-haired babe after another. She would take up embroidery and table decorating, or whatever it is matrons do with their days. But count on it—she will also take to drinking in the closet and gossiping with the maids out of sheer boredom. That clear-eyed doe will soon be an indolent old badger."

Darcy snorted. "What know you of women, Richard? The light-skirts who follow the drum, the maids who pour your ale, and your ill-tempered wife have taught you little about a true lady's character."

Richard cracked the balls together and straightened. "I know a bloody bit more than you, if you think you can marry her off to Bingley and be done with it."

Darcy leaned against his cue. "It does me little good to disagree with you, for the matter is out of my hands. Bingley has declared himself in love with Miss Jane Bennet, and unless he should alter his intent, it is she to whom he means to return."

"Ah. Then that does present a problem, for you will continue to have a remarkably handsome widow about. But, if she has any sense, she will rather marry after her mourning period ends than continue as Georgiana's companion. Only four more months, if I am not mistaken? I suppose you know some other chap in want of a wife." He finished his remarks with that Cheshire Cat grin of old days, a head tipped forward in interest, and a hand cocked at his hip.

Darcy slowly lowered his cue. "I see that marriage has not dampened your thirst for intrigue and gossip."

"A man needs some entertainment, and heaven knows I do not find it at home. I wonder, since you are so experienced in arranging the unions of others, have you a second gentleman in mind for Mrs Wickham? You must have given the matter some thought."

Darcy's only response was a grunt as he considered the table.

"A shopkeeper? Or perhaps a genteel farmer? She is not of the finest stock, if I recall correctly, but she has ample... assets. I trust you can warrant her... ah... quality?"

"Do not be such a pig, Richard," Darcy growled. "Whatever has got into you, speaking of an honourable widow as if she were merchandise? I begin to think you merely mean to irritate me."

His cousin merely shrugged and chuckled. "I have missed you, too, Darcy."

E LIZABETH'S FINGERS CRUSHED THE flower stem abruptly, bending it until the petals drooped. She turned her hand over and stared at it from all angles—noting the irony of that plain gold band she still wore, pressed against a dead bloom. How very fitting!

She ought to discard the ridiculous ring. It never meant anything in the first place, save for... well, the person who had slid it onto her finger. But that odd memory was gone the way of this poor flower. The autumn iris, so alive a moment ago, now looked as if it had been wilting for some days. Elizabeth sighed and cast it back into the flower beds before resuming her aimless wandering of the garden.

"Does not Mr Darcy object?" came a voice behind her.

Elizabeth turned to find Anne Fitzwilliam—pale under her wide bonnet and attended by a vigilant maid carrying an extra shawl. She curtsied. "I am uncertain what you can mean, Mrs Fitzwilliam. Do you mean to ask if he objects to my plucking a flower, or causing disarray among the hedges by discarding it so haphazardly? Or perhaps he might object to the muddy portion of grass I have just walked through, where some careless gardener spilled too much of the water that had been intended for a sapling? You are perfectly right, for I suppose he would object to my footprints ruining the sod and the sod spoiling my shoes."

The lady came near with a hawkish expression. "I heard you were an impertinent one, but you would do well to recall your place, Mrs Wickham. What I meant to ask, before you so flippantly presumed upon my intent, was whether your employer would object to you gadding about the grounds—alone and indecorously heedless of your appearance." She sniffed and appeared to take pleasure in staring at a bit of grass on Elizabeth's skirt before frowning and speaking once more. "Oughtn't you to make yourself decent and return to Miss Darcy?"

"Your concern is well-meant, I am sure," Elizabeth answered lightly. "Perhaps it is not so long that you cannot recall what it was to be a girl yourself—always some guardian or chaperon at your side? I have no desire to make myself an odious presence by over-constancy."

Mrs Fitzwilliam's cheek flinched. "I recall perfectly," she retorted in a frosty voice. "But Miss Darcy's preferences must and should be subject to her guardian's wishes."

Elizabeth bowed her head. "If Mr Darcy should make his objections known to me, I will be certain to address them. Good day, Mrs Fitzwilliam."

"Here, now! I have not taken my leave of you, Mrs Wickham. Do you dare to turn your back on me?"

Elizabeth looked over her shoulder, her expression all innocence. "Forgive me, Mrs Fitzwilliam, but when I said, 'Good day,' that was me taking my leave. Is that not how it is done in Kent?"

Anne Fitzwilliam's face took on the first hint of colour since Elizabeth had met her—though splotchy red could hardly be deemed healthy or attractive. "You take your leave of... A lady's companion dismissing me? Preposterous! Come back here, you!"

Elizabeth gritted her teeth and faced the woman once more. "I am a respectable widow with property of my own, madam."

"But who is your mother? A daughter of trade, no doubt, if her child possesses such audacity and so little decorum. I wonder at Mr Darcy for choosing such a—"

"Saucy minx? Poor influence? Provacateur?" A masculine voice interrupted Mrs Fitzwilliam, causing her to pale and jerk her head to the speaker. Mr Darcy himself had just rounded the hedge and was standing in his typical manner—hands clasped lightly behind his back, head inclined in half-facetious interest, and one foot slightly to the fore, as if to suggest that he was by no means on his guard. He glanced at Mrs Fitzwilliam, then turned his gaze to Elizabeth.

"Perhaps you are right, Anne," he mused with a half-smile. "Mrs Wickham is certainly all these things and is a dreadful choice as a proper companion."

"Precisely!" the lady agreed with energy. "Now, Darcy, if you would only look at the names I gave you last year, I am sure—"

"I have not done, Anne. Mrs Wickham?"

Elizabeth blinked and reached unconsciously to gather her skirt. "Yes?"

Mr Darcy gestured impatiently. "We had matters to discuss, had we not? You appear to be at your leisure and, at present, so am I." He turned to his cousin, giving her a formal bow. "Anne. I hope you enjoy the rest of your constitutional."

Elizabeth hesitated, but then a prick down her spine seemed to urge her forward. She fell meekly into step beside her employer, her body curved away from his as they walked side by side in an uncomfortable display of professionalism. She knotted her fingers in front of her stomach and fastened her eyes to the grass.

"I know what you wished to speak of," she offered in a flat voice.

"Do you? Then you know more than I."

"You are seeking some other arrangement for Miss Darcy—another companion, or perhaps she is to live with Lady Matlock to prepare for her coming out."

Mr Darcy frowned, but did not look at her. "That was not my intent."

"But you must see how much sense it makes," she protested. "We have not been without our troubles, and with a background such as mine, I can be of no credit to her—why, you heard what Mrs Fitzwilliam said."

He looked quizzically at her. "Why should either of us care what she said?"

"Because it is the truth!"

Mr Darcy pushed his lower lip out in a thoughtful, dubious expression wholly incongruous to his typical bearing. "And? It is also true that Anne Fitzwilliam made a scandalous dalliance by which she meant to force me to the altar, just to save her reputation. I should think the truth of your past is not nearly so tarnished as hers, and you see that I have not shunned my cousin."

"Because she is your cousin. I am no one."

Mr Darcy spun suddenly on the ball of his foot, his colour high and eyes curiously ablaze. "I will thank you never to repeat that, Mrs Wickham. Whatever you are, you are not no one."

She felt her own features paling as he fairly stared her into surrender. And, for the first time in their acquaintance, she wished herself to be in the wrong and him in the right. She could find no proper response, so she dropped her eyes and mumbled a "Yes, sir."

He held her in his gaze for another moment, almost daring her to some display of defiance. Twice, she hesitantly met his look, and then faltered.

"Very well," he sighed at last. He glanced over his shoulder, and still seeing Anne Fitzwilliam not far away, he steered her gently towards the orangery. "Tell me about your concerns. What can I do?"

She stopped, causing him to turn back to her. "So easy as that? You are not asking me to prove my case or defend my decision to ask for your help?"

"Why would I ask such a thing? Had I no confidence in you, I would never have chosen you for the roles I asked you to play."

Elizabeth regarded him carefully. He seemed to be in earnest.

"You were troubled on your sisters' account?" he prodded.

"Yes," she confessed. "Not that anything improper has taken place, but I wonder if Mr Wickham means to gain something by his displays of friendship. My family suspect nothing—even Jane, for she can only think well of people."

"You are asking me to reveal his infamy to your family? Regale your sisters with tales of his exploits?"

Elizabeth glared at him. "Of course not!"

"Then perhaps you wish me to have him shot when next he shows his face? I am afraid his crimes do not merit that."

"No, I—" She hissed in exasperation, then narrowed her eyes when she discovered the hint of a smile playing at his mouth. "You are provoking me again, sir."

His lips turned up in earnest, then his expression became grave once more. "Forgive me, Mrs Wickham. I found the opportunity too tempting to resist, but you have asked a serious question and I will not mock you. What is your true concern? That he means to work upon your sisters until he compromises one of them in revenge?"

She shrugged. "Perhaps. With Lydia, it is not unlikely that he might succeed, but I feel like he wants something else besides."

Mr Darcy frowned, then with a flick of his eyes gestured that he wished to resume walking. Elizabeth fell into step beside him as he spoke. "I had heard something while I was in London. From my uncle, Lord Matlock, if you wish to know. A source informed him that someone was legally challenging Bernard's legitimacy, and I think we both know who it was."

Elizabeth laced her hands tightly as she walked. "Can such a complaint succeed? Is there proof?"

Mr Darcy made no immediate reply. He studied the ground, his cheek twitching occasionally as if he were considering what answer he might make. "Possibly," he said at last.

"And if it did..." Elizabeth bit her lip and turned her face quickly away. She had taken for granted how comfortable it was to have a home, and to know her family were together and safe. If she lost Corbett, where would they go? She composed her features, but her voice was unsteady when she spoke again. "If it is not my right to hold the property, then it is not. But I thought you said your father designed the inheritance for Bernard? That all had been done legally?"

"It is true... to a point. But just as I did not pursue George Wickham when he wronged Anne or Georgiana, in the interests of protecting their honour, so my father left certain loose threads in the placement of Bernard."

Elizabeth was watching his expression—the hesitation, the pain never before witnessed, and she fought an impulse to touch his shoulder in a show of comfort. "I do not understand," she asked gently.

"Do you not? Is it so difficult for you to understand how easily a woman's life can be ruined by a rogue?"

"No, of course not. But what is that here?" She tilted her head and this time, she did dare to touch his arm because she could not stop herself. "Who was Bernard, really?"

Mr Darcy thinned his lips. "My mother's son."

Sixteen

"IT HAPPENED AFTER MY mother and father were betrothed. At a dinner party..."

Darcy led Elizabeth to the stone garden bench, allowing her to settle herself facing in one direction while he dropped down to it from the other.

"Your father knew?"

"He could not help it. When he and my uncle discovered her in the library, her gown was torn, and she was weeping inconsolably. She refused to name the scoundrel, but they knew very well that it had to be Lord Dewhurst."

"Oh..." Elizabeth's brow was contorted, her cheeks drawn. "Your poor mother!"

Darcy watched her steadily. Seated oppositely as they were, she was looking beyond him, but he could see each delicate vein of her neck, each indignant flicker of her cheek. "There was nothing to be done. Dewhurst was already married—not that anyone would wish to force my mother to break her engagement with a man she loved to marry her attacker. My uncle offered to pay my father to go forward with the marriage, an offer which my father adamantly refused, for he loved my mother deeply and would never have cast her off."

"So, what did he do?"

Darcy set his teeth and nodded as he recalled the tale. "What any respectable man would. He challenged Dewhurst on the field of honour. And won, I might add. Then he demanded that Dewhurst would provide for the child, for it was not to inherit Pemberley. My uncle helped to force this point, as the Matlock family hold considerable power in the House of Lords. Dewhurst finally agreed, and my father used the funds to purchase Corbett."

She turned to face him at last, those dark eyes nearly liquid with regret and sympathy. "And her child never knew her?"

"No. He was kept near, so that my mother would have the comfort of seeing her son, but for him to know her was not possible. Even old Wickham only knew that the child was the natural born son of 'someone,' but not whom. The only persons who knew Bernard's true parentage were my father, my uncle, and later myself. Dewhurst had every reason to conceal his part in it, for his financial humiliation was complete."

"But surely," she reasoned, "it is not impossible that someone might have said something, after all this time. A servant, even, might have known something."

He nodded slowly. "No one at Pemberley knew of it, because my parents took an extended wedding tour to Scotland. When the child was born, he was sent to old Wickham in secret, and my parents did not return for another two months. Dewhurst no longer lives, but he had an heir who might have learned something. So, I ask you; is it more likely that someone has suddenly given information, or that George Wickham wishes me to think someone has done so? He knows me, and he knew my father. He would know there is a stone somewhere to overturn regarding Bernard's identity, and he might just be daring enough to claim that he has found it."

She turned away and pursed her lips, her eyes unfocused on the trees overhead. "What would he gain by merely harassing you? Surely, if he has gone so far as to issue a legal complaint, he must have some proof."

"That is my instinct as well," he confessed. "And if Wickham did discover Bernard's true parentage..." A sickening realisation hit his stomach at that moment. Not for his family's tarnished honour, not for Georgiana's innocence, but for the woman seated at his side—the woman he had already forbidden himself to touch, because she was his brother's widow.

"I must leave," she finished in a flat voice. "I understand, sir. You have been very kind, but if my family cannot remain at Corbett, we will go elsewhere."

He did not correct her misapprehension—could not dare. Some part of him had clung to the idle thought that perhaps, if he could somehow settle it with his conscience, he might have had a future with her. And perhaps, if she continued to soften towards him as she had begun, she might have desired the same. But if the fact of Bernard's parentage was legally and publicly known, any such hope was dashed.

"I must speak with my steward," he announced at length. "I am also expecting my solicitor."

She looked back to him and swallowed, then nodded. "Yes. Shall I go to Miss Darcy?"

He gazed long into her eyes, then stared down at her fingers—at that wedding ring—as he lectured himself, once again, that she was not for him. "No," he answered softly. "Go to your family. Assure yourself that all is well and send word if you have need of anything."

She was looking down at his hands now too, but at last their eyes met. "Thank you, sir."

"E GAD, DARCY. DO YOU know, I always knew your father had hushed up Bernard's parentage for some reason, but this…" Richard made a low whistling sound. "I suppose that means Bernard was as much my cousin as you are. I feel soiled by the association," he said with a faint sneer of distaste.

"And well you might. Richard, I would not have Georgiana hear of this unless it cannot be helped. She always nursed some pity for Bernard, and that is enough in my mind. If she knew that our mother had suffered so, it would trouble her greatly."

"Right. So, what shall it be for Wickham? An 'accident,' or shall I just have the blackguard thrown into prison?"

"Do not be ridiculous, but I must know what information he has. I just spoke with my solicitor, and he is making inquiries. If there truly is evidence, I must be prepared."

"Suppose there is not? George was no more an heir of the body than Bernard was, so why would he truly open such a challenge if what he wants is Corbett? What if he is just performing his usual sleight of hand while he tries some other means behind your back?"

Darcy smiled. "Then I shall be grateful to have you here. What have you learned so far?"

"Only that he told the Bennet family he was bound for London."

Darcy paced before the mantel, tapping the leg of his trousers in thought. "I ordered my men to find Mrs Younge and Mrs Godfrey—or, rather, Isabella Wickham. Perhaps they will know something."

"For a price. How long, Darcy?"

"Hmm? How long what?"

Richard stepped near, shaking his finger. "How long do you mean to keep cleaning up after the Wickhams? Bribing and shepherding them into rectitude, settling their debts, mending the path of destruction in their wake?"

Darcy threw a hand in the air in exasperation. "What would you have me do? You see what he has done, whom he has harmed. You were bitter at me after I got you to wed Anne, but can you think of a happier resolution?"

Richard grumbled, rolled his eyes and drummed his fingers on the desk. "No," he admitted through clenched teeth. "It is not as if I expected to hold any special affection for the lady if I ever married, and I needed a bride with a fortune."

"Precisely. Anne's needs and yours were both satisfied, and the family honour preserved. Yet, if I had not nearly forced the issue, can you say it would have come about?"

"You are deliberately avoiding my point, Darcy. What of Wickham? He has gone from one offence to another for years, and will continue to do so as long as you pick up the pieces."

Darcy looked towards the window. "You know why I cannot confront him openly. Georgiana's reputation—"

"A pitiful excuse. Why not do as you did with Bernard and send him to prison?"

Darcy rose from the desk with a hiss. "He has been shrewder in his debts. I searched last autumn but discovered very little of use."

"And you did not ask me for help?"

Darcy cocked an eyebrow at his cousin. "If I recall correctly, you were still threatening to knock me down if I came near."

Richard stroked his jaw in thought. "Oh, yes. I would have helped you back up, you know."

Darcy offered a sort of laugh, then a knock came at the door. At Darcy's summons, the footman opened it and announced a harried, red-faced Bingley.

"Ah, there you are," Darcy greeted him. "I had almost given you up. You remember Richard, of course."

Bingley spared a short nod for Fitzwilliam, then came forward. "Darcy, I have just come from Corbett. Something dreadful has happened!"

The room turned cold, and Darcy's stomach twisted in dread. "Mrs Wickham? Is she injured?"

"No, no, it is Miss Lydia. She has disappeared!"

"Miss Lydia?" Darcy repeated. "When did this happen?"

"This afternoon, they said. I rode by—just a bit of a detour before coming here," he confessed with an abashed look. "Miss Jane met me in the drive, saying that Miss Lydia had gone, and Mrs Wickham is out going round to all the farmhouses looking for her. I came here as quickly as I could."

"I feared that one would be trouble," Darcy answered tightly. "I will come at once." Fitzwilliam was already at the door of the study, calling for his hat and coat. Darcy and Bingley followed close on his heels.

D ARCY FOUND MRS BENNET in a fit of hysterics to rival any thrown by his most flamboyant aunts. She greeted the search party from her sofa, a lace handkerchief fluttering about her ample bosom as her middle daughter strove to keep a vial of salts before her ever-wandering face.

"What has become of her?" she lamented. "My poor sweet Lydia, my innocent girl!"

"When did you last see her?" Darcy asked for the third time. "Was she here at luncheon?"

"Oh! I hardly know, I am in such a bad way. Lizzy would know, but she has gone off too, and for all I know they are both carried away to heaven knows what kind of fate. My poor girls! How could they do this to me?"

Miss Bennet sighed and spoke the first words of sense Darcy had heard since coming to the house. "Lydia was here at breakfast, but she asked for a large basket to be packed for a picnic. I heard nothing of this until later, but the kitchen girl did as she asked. I hardly know how Lydia could have carried it, if it was as full as Millie claims. Lydia told Kitty she was going walking with Lizzy, but then she told Lizzy that she was going out with Kitty. We knew nothing until luncheon when she did not return, for Lydia never misses a meal, and she is too addle-headed to embark on anything more than a quarter-mile walk."

"Has she any friends among the villagers?"

Miss Bennet pressed her lips together. "She would never go with us when we took baskets round, so I do not believe so."

Darcy caught Bingley's eye, for the latter had drawn close to his lady and was standing protectively behind her. "Where has Mrs Wickham gone, do you think?"

Miss Bennet gestured helplessly. "I expect she has been almost everywhere by now. I do not know where to tell you to look for her, but perhaps we may hope that she has discovered Lydia somewhere, and they are even now on their way back."

"Of course," Bingley agreed. "Why, that is precisely how it must be. Miss Lydia cannot have gone far, and Mrs Wickham is most resourceful."

Darcy fought a roll of his eyes as the happy couple consoled one another with this naïve hope. "Fitzwilliam," he announced to the glowering presence at his side, "I will ride west."

DARKNESS WAS FALLING RAPIDLY, and his sense of dread was escalating by the moment. Nearly two miles from Corbett Lodge, he dropped into a small valley where one of her tenants lived. It was the Smiths, a couple of advancing age with no children to attract a girl of fifteen to their home. Elizabeth would have left this as nearly the last house to search on her path, if he knew her as he thought he did.

His hammering heart and searching eyes were rewarded only a moment later when a woman's figure emerged from the trees. Her steps were faltering, her head down in defeat, and her gown splattered and stained from her exertions. Darcy nearly threw himself from his horse and ran to her.

"Elizabeth! Are you hurt?"

She scarcely raised her bonnet—merely shaking it back and forth as she crossed her arms over her chest. Darcy heard a sob, and it tore through his heart.

"Elizabeth!" He reached her and clasped her shoulders, unnerved by the way her form slackened and she refused to look him in the eye.

"It is my fault," she kept repeating. "I ought to have watched her better! I knew she would—oh, Mr Darcy, it is my fault!"

Darcy stripped off his riding coat and wrapped it about her against the evening chill. She shrugged into it as if grateful for the warmth, but still she would not lift her head.

"What can you mean, 'your fault,'?" he asked.

"I feared she would do something foolish! Please, Mr Darcy, you must leave me. We are ruined, all of us! You cannot be seen with—"

"Elizabeth," he interrupted. "Look at me."

She closed her eyes firmly, but slowly lifted her tear-streaked face to him.

"Much better. Now, I pray you tell me what has happened."

She drew a long, trembling sigh and nearly sobbed again. "I spoke with a farm maid who saw a girl who looked like Lydia. She was going south, they said—on the back of some man's horse."

Seventeen

"**M**r Darcy, this is intolerable. I must be allowed to return to my family!" Elizabeth sensed that she must have been exceedingly red in the face and her voice was becoming shrill with panic and fury, but it no longer mattered. What could Mr Darcy be to her now? What of it, if he now found her so repulsive and shrewish that he could scarcely abide the sight of her? Lydia must be her only concern, for it was not as if she would ever see him again after this.

If only he had not insisted on putting her on his horse and holding her in his arms for the ride back.

He would brook no refusal. "I understand your urgency, but you can serve your youngest sister better at Pemberley."

"You have said that thrice now, but I do not understand how my failure to return home at such a time will improve matters!"

"Why, do you not see? Your home is not safe until we discover where your sister has gone."

"Not safe! What do you suppose will happen? Shall a group of moustachioed brigands arrive with pistols and demand our immediate surrender?"

"Not unlikely," he answered, with no trace of irony in his voice.

"Oh, you are impossible. Pray, sir, let me return to my mother! I can imagine what a state she must be in."

"Even your imagination would fail to capture the full marvel of her histrionics," Darcy answered drily. "Not to worry, I will have her notified of your safety and a guard posted at Corbett until your family can be ready to remove."

Elizabeth stiffened. "It is come to that, then?" she asked in a tight voice.

"Naturally, anything else would be inconceivable. Your family cannot continue on there after these events."

Elizabeth turned her face as far away from his as she could manage—which was not very far. Tears burned, sobs welled up from within, but she would not release them. That the world would know of the family's disgrace and they would now be turned out seemed a paltry matter compared to the real pain in her heart—that Lydia might be lost to her forever, and Mr Darcy was even more so.

His arms tightened about her waist as he drew rein—it had nothing to do with her, she knew. It was merely the demands of managing his mount. But for half a moment, she wished it was sympathy or something deeper that made him seem to rock her body against his, to sigh against her cheek as he slowed the horse.

"We should dismount," was his gruff explanation. "We are within sight of the house."

She nodded half-heartedly. Nothing mattered now.

Except that it mattered very much when he vaulted to the ground behind her and then drew her down, cradling her in his arms. Was he clinging to her as he lowered her feet to the ground, or was he merely being considerate of her comfort when he let her down so slowly?

She hesitated, her eyes fixed on his splattered boots. "Thank you," she mumbled reluctantly.

His chest rose in a deep breath, held, and then he responded with a rigid, "Of course. Come, we cannot arrive too soon."

An army of footmen awaited them, with maids following closely behind to sweep Elizabeth into the house. Distantly, she heard Mr Darcy giving orders that she was to have a hot bath and tea, and then he addressed the coachman about sending out riders. The last words she heard before being ushered upstairs were "We must not let this be known until the Bennets have removed from Corbett."

Mr Darcy had an odd way of shunning a ruined family. Elizabeth hurried down to the drawing room that evening when the maid gave her the report that her mother and sisters had been brought to Pemberley. Not a cottage, not a coaching inn on the way back to London—no, they arrived in Pemberley's entry hall in a flurry of lace and tears and loudness and very nearly turned the great house upside down in all their effusions and distress.

Elizabeth had spent the intervening time packing her belongings. No one had said she must, and Miss Darcy even protested, but it was the only reasonable course. All the gowns had been provided by Mr Darcy, and it would not be right to keep them—however, there was that one with walking stains and a slight rip from the hedges, and surely he would not mind if she kept just that one. She might mend it to look respectable when she sought other employment, and she could pay him for it later if he insisted. The one travelling bag she had placed beside the door looked pitifully small compared to the trunk that had arrived with her, but at least she had felt honest.

Now, she was truly confused. She stood in the midst of the drawing room as her mother wept upon her shoulder, and Kitty marvelled at the furnishings. Mary was wide-eyed, and Jane looked pale and fragile in the great room, despite Mr Bingley coming to ask after her comfort every other minute. Even Georgiana had joined the mayhem, going from one sister to the next in a vain effort at hospitality and consolation.

"Oh, Lizzy, it is the most dreadful thing ever!" Mrs Bennet mourned. "Our poor Lydia, did you hear? Fallen ill so suddenly! My dearest child! Speak to Mr Darcy, will you? That beast of a man would not let me to my own daughter, though I am perfectly sure he knows in which house she lays. What do I care for falling ill myself when my baby is so sick in a strange house? As if some farmer could care for my daughter as she deserves!"

"Mama..." Elizabeth pried herself free of her mother's tearful embrace so she could look at Jane. "I do not understand. What are you speaking of?"

"Why, it is the scarlet fever, I just know it! Your Mr Darcy did not say as much—how very like a man! It is that or consumption, it simply must be. My child is at death's door, and I am not permitted to see her! You see how meanly he treats me, for he would not even allow me to remain at our own house, lest I go out on my own to search for her."

"I am sure that is not why he brought you here," Elizabeth answered with a long-suffering sigh.

"Speak to him, will you, Lizzy? He listens to you."

"Mama, I do not..." She broke off when Mr Darcy himself appeared at the door and bowed to her mother.

"Mrs Bennet, I have asked Mrs Reynolds to prepare rooms for you and each of your daughters. You will be shown up and made comfortable at once. If there is anything you desire, you have but to say the word."

Elizabeth watched him with a furrowed brow. Where was the man who was so anxious to rid the area of her family's scandal? He shifted his gaze to her and merely flicked his eyes to the right—as clear a direction as any he had ever given. Then he bowed and went out.

"Excuse me, Mama," Elizabeth said breathlessly.

"Yes, yes, follow him, Lizzy. Find out where my Lydia is!"

"I DO NOT KNOW where your sister is."

Elizabeth paced around to face him where he stood near the window. "Why did you tell my mother that she was an invalid in someone's house?"

"I should have thought it obvious. Until we have better information, there is no reason to bring scandal upon your family. It may be that it is not yet too late."

"Too late! It was too late the moment she walked out of the house with that picnic basket. I know very well that she must have intended to meet someone. It was all arranged beforehand! If only I had not trusted her—oh, it is my fault!"

Mr Darcy's arms were crossed, and he had been leaning towards the window, but at her last utterance he rounded upon her.

"Your fault? Was it your fault when you sacrificed yourself to give your family a home?"

She looked away. "I hardly sacrificed mys—"

"What was it then, when you trusted your future to a stranger? When you let yourself be wed to a diseased wretch to provide for your mother? When you lowered yourself to a life of service—howbeit a temporary one—to make a home for your sisters?"

Elizabeth's jaw was tight, and her nostrils distended with the effort of maintaining her composure. "It was you yourself who did all the providing."

"Yet you maintained your end of the bargain with faith and diligence. None could consider any of this your fault, Elizabeth."

She lifted her chin. "Why do you insist on calling me by my Christian name, sir?"

He blinked. "My apologies if I have offended. At such a time, I preferred—and I thought you would as well—not to recall your legal surname. What other reason could I have?"

Elizabeth heaved a weary sigh and turned away in search of a chair to sink into. "Oh, I do not know. I suppose my mind has conceived all manner of paranoid fantasies. I know very well that my... my former husband's name and inheritance are suspect—"

"The legality of your marriage as well."

"What?"

Mr Darcy offered a weak smile and carefully took the nearest seat. "If anyone wanted to contest it, that is. The parson was none too happy with the proceedings, and it was not later legitimised by... well. I think that ought to be the last of our concerns at the moment."

Elizabeth groaned and dropped her face into her palms. "You still think George Wickham is at the root of all this?"

Mr Darcy cleared his throat, all business again. "Yes. I have sent riders out to every coaching inn and farmhouse for fifty miles. They will have fresh mounts, and they will cover the ground quickly. However, I doubt they will find our elusive couple. Wickham gains nothing without making demands, sending threats. He will be hiding somewhere nearby, and I should be astonished if we do not have a note from him before dawn."

"And then what? They discover my sister ruined in some cottage?"

He closed his eyes, and when he opened them, they were filled with such pain and empathy that she saw, for the first time, the depth of the man within. "Let us pray it has not yet come to that."

Eighteen

T HE NOTE CAME PRECISELY at midnight. The young lad who had received a shilling to carry it could not tell the present whereabouts of the sender, but no one needed to ask him the man's identity. Darcy took it from the footman with a grim scowl and read it at once. His expression never flickering, he passed it not to Colonel Fitzwilliam, who stood by like a seething ogre, but to Elizabeth.

"It is certain, then. Wickham has the aid of either Mrs Younge or his mother, likely both, and has secured Miss Lydia against potential escape. Richard, did not the riders who returned from East Orchards report that the former Mrs Wickham's abode was vacant?"

"Yes, as well as that of the erstwhile 'Mrs Brown,' or Mrs Younge as was. They would know we would search there first for that vermin."

Elizabeth had finished reading Wickham's note and was swaying slightly, her features pale like glass. "He offers to marry her if I deed Corbett to him? How can I not agree? And yet, if I do, to what sort of fate have I consigned my sister? She is but fifteen!"

Darcy put a hand on her shoulder, his thumb nearly grazing her soft cheek. "You will do no such thing. I'll not have Wickham established nearly on my front lawn, and I will not see him ruin yet another young woman or turn you out of your home."

"But it is too late! He as much as said in the note—" She wrung the offending paper and crushed it to her forehead as loud gasps shook her. "She is lost! I know very well that nothing good can come of this."

Darcy's hand lifted hesitantly from her shoulder, and he glanced at Richard. It was only they three in the room, for everyone had been persuaded to bed, save for Elizabeth who had adamantly refused. Richard caught Darcy's look of frustration and deliberately turned away. Darcy followed the sound of his heavy steps as he left the room and barked out orders for his horse.

"Elizabeth." He touched her back, coaxing her to draw near until her bowed head leaned against his shoulder. "We will find her. Even should it be as we suspect, we may yet be able to restore her. Come, my dear—"

She stiffened, raising her head and staring at him as if he were a stranger. "Mr Darcy, do not speak thus. Pray, be rational about this, as I have come to depend on you as a man of reason. I cannot bear false hope at such a time."

All the warmth of feeling welling up in his breast crashed into icy pain as he lowered his hand once more. "You are perfectly right," he confessed, though his voice cracked slightly.

"Do we even know how to search for her? Can there be any way of knowing?"

"We have men searching the entire countryside. Fitzwilliam and I mean to ride out at once, now that we have a hint of his intentions. We both have our grievances to settle, but Wickham had better pray that I find him before my cousin does."

She swallowed tightly and dashed a few tears from her eyes before offering him the rumpled note. "Will this help?"

He took it, but his attention was all for her. "Elizabeth, we will find her. Your mother will have her daughter again."

She hugged herself, her shoulders hunched as she attempted a brave smile. "I hope so. Thank you, for all you have done. You owe us nothing, sir, but it will be a great comfort in the years to come when I look back on our time here in Derbyshire. Few are those who would do so much for someone so unconnected with themselves."

Darcy stiffened. "You are not 'unconnected,' you are... good heavens, you are my brother's wife, and mine to care for. Unpack that bag I know you have ready and get some sleep, or I will send Mrs Reynolds in to watch you every second."

She lowered her head, but a twitching, reluctant curve appeared at the edge of her lips. "I dare not disobey my employer. God speed, Mr Darcy."

"NO GIRL HERE," SEEMED to be the common refrain for ten miles around. Darcy and Richard had started off on different routes, but their paths crossed later in the afternoon and they completed the circuit together.

"Foolish strumpet," Fitzwilliam hissed after their last stop proved fruitless. "Stupid, thoughtless girl!"

"If she is," Darcy answered mildly, "others have been more so. She is but fifteen, Richard."

"Precisely! She ought to have been learning her embroidery or practising an instrument. What the devil could her mother have been about, not watching her every second?"

"The same thing as many others—desiring to allow her child a bit of liberty. Not all take to it well."

Fitzwilliam scoffed, then beat his arms to warm himself. "After I put the noose around Wickham's pretty little neck, I mean to see that girl locked away until she is forty and too old to run after stray men."

"If that satisfies your offended sense of justice. I must speak with my steward." Darcy urged his mount to a gallop, leaving his irascible cousin to express his outrages to none but his own horse.

The first faces to greet him upon his return to the house were the last he had desired to see. Anne Fitzwilliam and Lady Sophia appeared to be just returning from a stroll in the garden, and they waited for him in the entry hall.

"Darcy!" cried Lady Sophia as he came up the steps. "Why, you must be fearfully exhausted. You must have been out all day, have you not? And in this cold!"

"I have." He turned to offer his coat to the footman and proceeded into the house, but Lady Sophia would not be so easily brushed off. She followed close at his elbow, with Anne trailing not far behind.

"My dear cousin, let me call for some refreshment for you. Truly, you look exceedingly weary."

"I thank you, but I must speak to my steward." He bowed quickly, and turned away, but her hand at his shoulder stayed him.

"Will you not tell me what this is about?" She tilted her head and bestowed a sweet smile upon him, tossing her curls ever so slightly. "You arouse my pity by your long exertions and then refuse to be comforted. Poor form, my dear cousin!"

"I am afraid," said he, "that the matter is a private one."

"Private, he says!" she lamented to Anne. "Darcy, you have been too many years alone. A man in your position must learn to share a bit of his burden. Why, that is why you asked me here, was it not? To bring comfort and pleasure to the party—you said it yourself, so I must assume you meant every word, for you are nothing if not sincere."

He nodded impatiently. "Indeed. I presume you and Anne are a great comfort to one another."

"Oh, Darcy!" The lady affected a mournful sob. "How callous you are! You will not tell me what has become of that young Bennet girl, but I can imagine well enough. Why, the scandal, if it is learned that the sister of Miss Darcy's companion has fallen into disrepute! Truly, sir, you are too generous, expending your energies on a girl of no account as you have. No one could fail to credit you as a magnanimous master, but do you not think all this entanglement in that girl's affairs might be misconstrued?"

Darcy was staring incredulously at his cousin. "Misconstrued?"

"Why, naturally." She stepped close and trailed her eyes over his frame in a manner that could only be called possessive. "One can understand your desire to hush up any scandal before it can be widely known, but to oversee the affair personally? Secrete the mother and sisters in your own house?" She laughed gently. "It is not as if you are in any way beholden to that shameful family. Why not send them all away before any breath of suspicion may touch our dear Georgiana?"

Darcy took a careful step backwards. His gaze flitted to Anne, and to Richard, who was finally coming through the front door, before narrowing once more on Lady Sophia. "I am afraid it is you who have misconstrued matters, Cousin," he informed her. "As it happens, I am deeply invested in the welfare of the entire Bennet family."

She made a face of mock condescension. "Come, Darcy, you cannot be serious. I suppose you will claim it is all for the benefit of a certain lady's companion? Such creatures are to be found anywhere—why, 'twould be the work of a moment to secure a proper replacement for her."

Darcy permitted his teeth to show. "I am afraid not. Elizabeth Wickham is, apart from my own sister, the only female in this house who is irreplaceable."

A loud snort of appreciation from Richard accompanied his wife's horrified gasps. Darcy stared back at Lady Sophia just long enough to ensure that she was sufficiently silenced. Her complexion changed hues more than once, but the most satisfying bit was the way her elegant mouth gapped like a doomed fish. Darcy turned on his heel and marched down the hall...

Directly into Elizabeth.

"PLEASE, SIR, I AM not accustomed to explanations from you, nor did I ask for one." Elizabeth retreated to the far side of Mr Darcy's study and stood with her arms crossed.

Mr Darcy approached slowly, more hesitantly than his usual manner. "And I am not accustomed to the necessity of explaining myself. You have always been clever enough that I need not feed you with a spoon, but under the circumstances, it would not be unreasonable if you had a question or two."

"I have several dozen, but only a few of them are pertinent at the moment." She cast her eyes to the ceiling and bit her lip.

He stood before her now, his hands first on his hips, then clasped behind his back, then gesturing in wordless frustration. "Allow me to assume the first, then. It... it came to my attention that my cousin, Lady Sophia, may have cultivated certain expectations. Expectations that I have no intention of satisfying."

"I am sure your personal affairs are no business of mine, sir."

His brow fell. "Have you no questions at all about the conversation you heard?"

Elizabeth drew in a breath and looked away. "You believe that I have."

"I hope you have... no, I can see it for myself. You are blushing, Elizabeth."

She turned back, her eyes wide. "Do you delight in humiliating me, sir?"

He shook his head. "No."

"Then you find pleasure in provoking me?"

"Immensely, but not in the way you expect." He waited for some retort, some display of indignation... but she could summon none.

He edged closer but stopped when she looked up. "I am a rascal, I suppose—always seeking a way to make your fine eyes flash and your courage flame. I admire your bravery and your spirit, and how all my arrogance never intimidated you."

Elizabeth tried to laugh, but it came as something of a sob. "Never, you think?"

He narrowed his eyes. "Elizabeth? Have I given you pain?"

"Pain? You have made me wonder every moment I am in your presence what you are truly thinking. Sometimes I believe I can make sense of your ways. I think you are a—a pragmatic sort of man with a multitude of idiosyncrasies designed to conceal a naturally generous spirit, but that is all. Then, just when I believe myself to understand you, you turn about and declare thoughts and intentions that a man of your position has no business harbouring. And the very next moment, you harden once more and that glimpse I thought I saw of something—someone—else has vanished. How am I not to feel constantly bewildered?"

"If either of us is bewildered by the other, it is I." He was studying her with a grave expression, his confident manner entirely gone. He made no answer for a full minute, but he drew a long breath and released it slowly. "Would you be so troubled by my manners if we were... say, if I were only Georgiana's guardian to you? An employer, no more?"

Elizabeth tried to speak, but her throat was too tight. She cleared it nervously. "I suppose not. But we are more than that, are we not, sir?"

"Are we? Have you some feeling for me, Elizabeth? I had persuaded myself that you could not have, and I even tried to convince myself that I had none for you, but the latter effort was unsuccessful. Was I wrong in the first as well?"

Elizabeth's skin grew hot, and she looked away, stammering out a barely coherent response. "Feeling! Why... improper—that would be most—what I mean, sir, is that we are... well, apart from you being my employer, we are neighbours, and r-relatives, and..."

"Are we friends, Elizabeth?"

She sucked in a breath, her lips quivering, and stared him in the eye. "F-friends. Yes, I... I think so."

His entire figure seemed to relax, either in relief or disappointment. "Friends," he whispered, then shook his head and sighed.

An instant later, he straightened and reclaimed his bearing. He turned from her and began to pace uncomfortably, glancing at her every few steps before he stopped and spoke. "As your friend, I must bring you the discouraging news that we have not yet had word of your sister."

Elizabeth closed her eyes. "I feared you would say this."

"I still have riders searching all the lands nearby, but there are simply too many houses and cottages. Even a cellar could conceal her, particularly if it has a lock."

A cellar! What horrors had Lydia endured? Elizabeth nodded, clenching a fist to her mouth as the tears began to pour afresh. She had been snarled amid fury at Lydia for her foolishness and fury with herself for her blindness, but now all she could feel was failure and despair. Her poor youngest sister—only a child! Elizabeth's body was quaking with sobs, and at last she broke. All the ugliness and horror of pain claimed her, and grief washed through her. She faltered, put her hand out blindly for something to lean against.

And then, she felt it. A firm shoulder, a strong arm about her; and Mr Darcy, who never lacked for an outrageous thing to say, silently held her to his chest as she wept. Patiently, gently, he allowed her to exhaust her grief, until she was sniffling and drawing back on her own. Even then, he gave her a handkerchief and waited in perfect solicitude as her tremblings subsided.

"Thank you," she managed in a broken voice.

"Do not give up hope. One of the last rumours we heard before returning was that Mrs Younge—you know her as Mrs Brown—was seen departing on a post chaise two days ago. She was reported to be alone."

Elizabeth was numbly biting down on the tip of her thumb as her eyes glazed over in thought. "Then it does not seem as if she would know where Lydia is?"

"Unless Wickham had intended to meet her en route somewhere."

"What of Mrs Godfrey?"

"Do you mean Isabella Wickham? No word at all, which surprises me not a bit. She was never one to stay in the same place."

Elizabeth squinted, then her eyes focused sharply on his face. "The first time I saw her, she was arguing with the innkeeper in Lambton. Is he her brother, as she claimed? Would she be hiding with him?"

Mr Darcy's brow furrowed. "Samuel Jameson is an honest man. I cannot think he would be party to any scheme to harm a young lady. We did ask at the inn, but the proprietor swore he had seen neither George Wickham nor a girl of your sister's description." His gaze strayed; his jaw hardened. "However, he does keep poultry, or rather his wife does. They have large shelter and yard not far from town. It would be worth looking there."

Nineteen

D ARCY WASTED NOT A minute of that afternoon. Immediately upon seeing Elizabeth comforted and returned to the solace of her room, Darcy called Bingley and Fitzwilliam into his study.

"We have been approaching this badly," he announced. "I am going to the inn for a drink."

Bingley looked blankly at Fitzwilliam, then back to Darcy. "What, are you giving up so soon? You would not try to help Jane's sister? By heaven, I will go search for her myself!"

Fitzwilliam crossed his arms and pointed with his chin. "That is precisely what he means for us to do, Bingley. Where shall we go?"

"Anywhere you like. One of the few places that I do not believe we have inspected is Jameson's poultry shed."

"And I presume that you will order an ale at the inn? Not quite your usual drink."

Darcy nodded. "No, but I expect I will be ordering more than one."

T HREE ALES LATER, DARCY set his empty glass back on the table with a bit more force than he had intended. His stomach was uneasy, and not only because of the assault he had just inflicted upon its lining. Mr Jameson himself came to the table when he saw the empty glass and offered another.

Darcy winced and shook his head. "Not at present, thank you," he declined.

"Of course, Mr Darcy." Jameson turned away, but hesitated. "If I may, Mr Darcy, it is a pleasure to have you as a guest. Are you sure I may not offer you a private room?"

"That will not be necessary. This entire half of the establishment is vacant at present."

The innkeeper's thick brow showed disappointment. "As you wish, sir. May I ask the name of the man you are waiting for, so I may direct him to you?"

"You know him already. George Wickham."

Jameson's countenance grew sallow and cold. "He's gone from these parts, and good riddance to the beggar. With all due respect, sir," he amended quickly.

"Nevertheless, I expect he will arrive shortly. I have changed my mind, Jameson—two more ales, if you please."

Jameson bowed his deference and shuffled away. Darcy watched him go, searching for any symptoms of a burdened conscience. The innkeeper whispered to a dustboy, but neither disappeared shortly afterward and none of the other customers suddenly got up to leave the room. The ales arrived in due course, and Darcy let them sit untouched for another quarter of an hour.

So idle and dull was the entire atmosphere that it was a struggle to keep his eyes open after the drinks. His gaze drifted to the clock and fixed there without truly seeing anything until the chair opposite him thumped and a body dropped into it.

"There is a remarkably fine hunter standing in the stable out back," Wickham remarked casually. He lifted the ale on his side of the table and took a long draught. "I thought you would have brought your carriage."

"As well as a lady to plead with you?" Darcy countered. "What I had to say to you could be said without inflicting your lies on another's ears."

Wickham made a sour face as he set the glass down. "You do delight in being a difficult bastard."

"On the contrary, my parentage is not suspect."

Wickham snorted. "As you bring the matter up, let us have it. You know I have proof of Bernard's birth. That is why you came so quickly back from London, is it not? The earl heard of my case, I presume."

Darcy lifted his shoulders. "What of it?"

"What will you give me to keep it quiet?"

"Nothing whatsoever."

Wickham stared, then laughed. "I see how it is! You expect me to tip my hand, but I will not do it. I have Lydia Bennet, and the wench thinks I mean to marry her. By challenging Bernard's legitimacy or by marriage to the sister, I will have what ought to have been mine. So, all that remains is for you to tell me which it shall be."

Darcy slowly sipped his drink and pretended to consider. "What I do not understand, Wickham, is why you would settle for Corbett when you could have had Pemberley."

Wickham blinked. "Come again?"

"Why, if you have legally valid proof of Bernard's true parentage, as you claim, then you would know by now that his widow could not, in fact, inherit Corbett. His claims were far higher, had he only known—the poor devil. And if, indeed, Bernard's widow is not your legal sister-in-law, why... but I am sure you had already thought of this."

Wickham's eyes were wide, and he coughed slightly but made an effort at recovering himself.

"It is a pity you fell for the wrong Bennet sister," Darcy informed him casually. "The youngest sister has no claims at all, but Elizabeth could be worth ten thousand a year, if your evidence is found to be compelling in court. There is no entail, as you are aware."

"Now, wait a minute, Darcy." Wickham wiped his mouth and held up a hand. "I never touched Lydia Bennet. I could have—the chit is as loose and silly as they come—but there was no time."

Darcy frowned and shook his head. "Too late for such a claim, I am afraid. If your demands succeed in court, Miss Lydia's sister will be a very powerful woman indeed, and you do know what they say about a woman's wrath."

"But I did nothing to her! She came searching for me! I only put her up somewhere safe—"

"Oh." Darcy shrugged again. "Then, I suppose there is no harm done. I will bid you a good day, then." He stood, tossed a few coins on the table, and started for the door.

"Wait a minute, Darcy!" came a half-petulant cry behind him. "I have not yet done. I have complaints—proofs!"

Darcy turned round and stared at the man who had been a bane to his adult years. "You have nothing. And, as you were so eager to believe the commonly held myth that my father sired Bernard—which is false, and even if it were true, he was still illegitimate—I know now that any 'proof' you claim to have is nothing more than a fabrication meant to divert me."

Wickham sputtered, then hastened to catch up with Darcy, kicking a few chairs from his path. "But I do have Miss Lydia! What have you to say to that, Darcy?"

Darcy opened the door leading out into the street, nodded to the man who stood just outside, and called for his horse. Wickham followed, pushing aside the door that nearly closed in his face, until he stumbled into the very man waiting on the step.

"George Wickham," Colonel Fitzwilliam growled. "I bring you greetings from my wife."

T HE ROUND VALLEY RANG with the scraping of steel upon steel. Darcy stood beside the horses, who placidly flicked their tails as they gazed disinterestedly at the two struggling men at the centre of the valley.

"You have grown old and fat, Fitzwilliam!" Wickham taunted—yet it was he who appeared to be battling the most for breath. Sweat beaded his forehead in the cool air, but he was too distracted to wipe it away.

"Try me and see if your blade will sink," Richard shot back. "You will find me a more difficult mark than the one whose honour I am here to avenge."

Wickham turned his head and spat as he bent forward, leaning his palms over his thighs in a momentary respite. "You do not even like the woman! Why all this fuss and bother over a spoilt heiress who—"

Wickham never finished his insult, for an enraged Richard Fitzwilliam barrelled down upon him and knocked him asunder with the brass hand guard of his sword hilt. Wickham lay back, dazed and bleeding from a missing tooth and a split lip, while Richard calmly cleaned his sword. Darcy remained where he was, leaning one arm against the mane of the nearest horse and examining his pocket watch.

"Do you submit?" Fitzwilliam demanded.

Wickham felt his jaw and visibly winced as he sat up. "Submit to what?"

Richard's blade caught the sun as he carefully turned it over—a bit of intentional theatrics, Darcy thought, but effective, nonetheless. Wickham closed his mouth.

"These are my terms, Wickham. Either you sign up at once with the next regiment to be deployed on the Continent, or I test the sharpness of my steel against the skill of your tailor. How well do you like the weave of your coat?"

Wickham swiped the blood from his chin and glared—first at Fitzwilliam, then at Darcy. "Are you in accord with this, Darcy? You would truly send a man to his death on the battlefield?"

Darcy replaced his pocket watch. "No. I would send you to prison, as soon as I had gathered your debts."

Wickham stared, as if expecting Darcy to recant his resolve, then tossed his sword on the ground at Fitzwilliam's feet. The oaths he uttered as he marched from the field of honour were scarcely fit even to be heard, much less repeated, so Darcy turned a deaf ear and merely prepared to mount his horse.

"I thought you meant to run him through." Darcy passed his cousin the reins to his chestnut as Richard walked back from the field.

Richard mounted with a grim expression. "No sport in slicing rodents. My dignity would suffer too greatly. Besides, I believe my second would object to cleaning up the body."

"I would have, yes. Better to let Napoleon teach our old friend a thing or two about valour."

Fitzwilliam settled into his saddle with a heavy groan. "If he even enlists, rather than leaving the country. What do you think, will he run to America instead?"

Darcy shook his head and turned his mount. "If he does, I hope he takes his mother. So long as he never troubles my family or yours again, I no longer care. What will Anne say?"

"Oh! She would not speak to me for a month if I told her. Remember, 'nothing ever happened,' so I will avenge the insult without her knowledge, thank you. Mayhap now, I will be able to look at her without hating myself for failing to do as I wished I had done before." He glanced thoughtfully up at the sky. "I could... you know, I just might."

"Might what?"

"Make a decent enough husband. I am not fooling myself into thinking we will develop any romantic feelings—such a thing is rarely to be found, though..." he gave Darcy a peculiar grin. "I have seen it once. Nevertheless, I expect we will rub along well enough. Who knows, I might even have a son one day. But I do think it time I took certain measures to ensure better harmony, and I shall begin by removing my wife and sister to Matlock on the morrow."

"To Matlock? I hope you know that you are still, and always shall be, most welcome at Pemberley."

"And I am most grateful, but it is time we began behaving as man and wife, not bickering cousins. Moreover, I expect your life might be simpler without Sophia about, am I right? My father and mother ought to have come away from London by now, anyway. And what do you mean to do?"

"To catch up to Bingley and Miss Lydia, of course. You said they departed for Corbett at once after the two of you found her? And he did send for the apothecary to keep up the illusion of her illness, did he not?"

"That is not what I was asking, Darcy. Wickham is dispatched, and if I have anything to do with it, Mrs Younge will be imprisoned on charges of 'lewd conduct' for her part in kidnapping Miss Lydia. Your fair lady and her family are safe."

Darcy refused to look at his cousin. "She is not 'my fair lady,' and never can be."

"What, because of your misguided sense of righteousness? To the world, she is Elizabeth Wickham, a handsome young widow in possession of a neighbouring estate whose mourning is soon to come to an end."

"And to me, she is the widow of my mother's son, and the property she holds ought never to belong to the Darcy name on the grounds of decency and honour."

Richard snorted. "I suppose you would have to work out your qualms about the property, but the bit about her being your brother's widow is a ridiculous law. Bernard is dead, for pity's sake, and that makes her no more your sister than I am. Moreover, she was never truly his wife, was she?"

Darcy's hands were rigid on the reins as he gritted his teeth and stared at the road. "Not in the way you mean, but in the eyes of the law she was."

"And in the eyes of the law, Bernard was not your brother. Come, Darcy, you cannot hide behind legal proceedings in one instance and not the other. I know bloody well that you fancy the woman. You can scarce tear your eyes from her, and she was nearly green with envy when I dropped a hint that you might marry—I let her believe you meant to wed my sister."

Darcy turned slowly. "She was?" He furrowed his brow and shook his head. "No, she could not have been. She informed me often... She was? Truly?"

"Green as grass, and almost ill to her stomach if I am any judge. You cannot truly confess now that you would stand on a flimsy excuse when the woman you admire returns your feelings, would you?"

Darcy's brow was sweating despite the chill air, and all his muscles were quivering. "That would be insupportable," he breathed.

"OH, MY SWEETEST CHILD! My dearest Lydia, how silly of you to fall ill when you were out walking," Mrs Bennet scolded her youngest. "Why, you look well enough to me, but you always did mend the fastest of anyone. How clever of Mr Darcy to let you recover in a neighbour's home, so you needn't have endured a cold ride when you were ill. Millie, some hot bricks for Miss Lydia's bed, and an extra cup of tea for Mr Darcy!"

Darcy shook his head as he backed from the room. "That will not be necessary, Mrs Bennet. I only came to see that Miss Lydia was recovering from her ordeal."

The girl herself raised a sullen pout to Darcy. She still smelt of a poultry house, but not a hair had been ruffled on her head, save for what she had done herself when Bingley had tried to pull her from Jameson's shed where she and Mrs Younge had been hiding. Her mouth opened to make some ill-tempered retort, but Darcy saw Elizabeth's chin lift and her eyes flash in warning to the younger girl. Miss Lydia frowned and mumbled a half-hearted gratitude.

"Think nothing of it," he replied. "Oh, Mrs Wickham, did I mention to you that I had the name of an excellent young lady's academy in Devonshire? The headmistress's letter assured me that she enforces the strictest order. I understand that the young ladies there spend four hours each day memorising Fordyce, four at their needlework or the pianoforte and the remaining four exercising humility by boiling the linens and scrubbing the floors."

Elizabeth slitted her eyes at him, as if trying to determine whether he was in earnest.

"Of course," he continued, "young ladies of good character and honourable station may be more comfortable remaining with their families under the instruction of a private tutor. I say, Mrs Wickham, my sister has been planning a trip to Town soon to be fitted for a winter wardrobe. She most particularly wished for one or two of your sisters to accompany her—if you have determined they have need of ball gowns, that is."

A curl appeared at the corners of Elizabeth's mouth. "We will consider these things, Mr Darcy. Lydia, dear, you look dreadfully pale! You ought to be in bed recovering, as the apothecary has said."

The girl was still staring gap-mouthed at Darcy but collected herself without a word and with little reluctance when her mother draped a heavy cloak round her shoulders and bundled her off up the stairs.

Elizabeth sighed as her mother and sister left. "I appreciate your threats and bribery, sir. Time will tell if Lydia heeds the warning not to speak another word of Mr Wickham. I have cautioned her, and so has Jane, but she seems not to understand the gravity of her error or the character of the man in whom she trusted."

"I have no doubts that you will prove the more obstinate and determined of the two of you." For the first time, Darcy let his gaze rest on her with unconcealed tenderness. "I will, of course, aid you in any way possible."

"First—" She turned up to him with an earnest look and stopped just short of touching his forearm. "I wish to know the truth of what happened—how you discovered her, and where Mr Wickham is."

He held out his hand towards the door. "If you will permit me to escort you on a short walk?"

She nodded and caught her shawl from a hook. He held the door for her, and then extended his elbow for her to take. She looked up at him doubtfully, but with a small smile she wove her arm through his.

"It is Richard and Bingley you have to thank for discovering her whereabouts. It seems that Mrs Younge had only appeared to leave the area, for she was securing the door of the poultry house when they arrived. After finding your sister safe, Richard met me as I was departing the inn with Wickham. A challenge was issued, fought, and Wickham has pledged on his rather dubious honour to join the Regulars."

She shivered, and he paused to adjust the wrap over her shoulders. "Do you think he will do it?"

"I think he would rather take his chances with Bonaparte's cannons than Richard's blade. Yes, I believe he will. I also believe we will not see 'Mrs Godfrey' again, as she can no longer expect anything from her son. I spoke with her brother Jameson at the inn after your sister was found in his poultry shed, and he was outraged that she had deceived and used him so badly. He has washed his hands of her and sent her away to some distant aunt."

"Then that is the end of it." She was gazing distantly over the fields, then turned her eyes back up to him. "And there is no longer any question of the disposition of Corbett Lodge?"

"None. It is yours for as long as you choose to live in it."

"Then I intend to give it to my mother. I cannot—I do not wish to call it my own. I hope that does not make me ungrateful."

He watched her profile in the fading light, but she held fixedly, not looking at him. "The decision is yours, but it is a wise one. I will assist with any legal matters you require."

She nodded slowly. "Thank you."

They said nothing more. There was so much Darcy longed to ask of her, to understand, but for the moment, it was enough simply to walk beside her in the gathering dark of evening. Each step, each breath carried meaning and perception, and the weight of her small hand on his arm was more to him than a hundred words.

By the time he brought her back to her door, it was too dark in the entry to determine if she was blushing, but the soft twist to her mouth and the teasing shift of her eyes assured him that she was. "Does Miss Darcy wish for my return on the morrow?" she asked.

He pretended to frown. "No. As a matter of fact, Mrs Wickham, your services shall no longer be required, and I must inform you that I have decided to terminate your employment."

Her eyebrows twitched. Once, she would have paled and stepped away, thinking only of how she had failed her family. Or, perhaps she might have argued with him, debating him into surrender on the grounds of justice and the virtue of keeping his word. Now, however, she only smiled.

"Excellent. I was going to give my notice anyway."

"Were you, now?"

She nodded once, allowing her gaze to rove over his face. "But if you wish to call as a neighbour, we are always happy to receive you, Mr Darcy."

He tipped his hat and bowed gallantly. "It is not impossible that you may see me tomorrow. Good evening, madam."

Twenty

E LIZABETH CLOSED THE DOOR behind herself as she set out after Jane and Mr Bingley. The lovers had decided upon a short walk on this autumn day, and the duty of chaperoning them fell happily to her lot. It was a far more pleasant task than that which had fallen to Mary—instructing a petulant Lydia on the pianoforte.

A few leaves crunched underfoot as Elizabeth strayed somewhat from the path taken by the couple ahead of her. The day was cool and crisp, and not unlike that day nearly a year ago, when she had peered timidly out of the door of a carriage to examine Corbett Lodge for the first time. She sighed in contentment, relishing the clean scent of winter coming and the earthy aroma of the land turning inward for slumber. And then, a second pair of footsteps joined her own. There was no unnecessary greeting, no callous touch—she simply felt, and he was there.

Fitzwilliam Darcy.

"I had hoped you might join us today," she said.

"I did threaten to come. Did you not believe me?"

She laughed and looked him full in the face. "Of course, I did, but that does not diminish the fact that I hoped for your company."

His mouth appeared ready to break into a smile, but he seemed to try to appear nonchalant. "Come, madam, you must be in jest. One does not hope for what one is sure of."

"On the contrary, I find that my hope is best served when it is set upon a secure foundation. From there, it may flourish, where a hope placed in something uncertain can do little but stretch until it is broken."

"And where is your hope, Elizabeth?"

She snapped off the stem of a tree as she passed it and idly twirled it about her fingers. "Here. Like a wild sapling cut from its native roots and then grafted into a new tree—here is my home and here are my people."

He stopped and turned towards her, stepping close. "Do you know, Elizabeth, that mind and tongue of yours have bewitched me from the first time I met you. You see things that I do not, and you can express in a simple phrase what I have tried to describe all my life."

Her cheeks warmed, and she looked down. "It is nothing. Merely the ramblings of a mind that no doubt wants for discipline and education."

"No one admitted to the pleasure of hearing you speak could think anything wanting."

She dared to meet his eyes. They were soft, now—warm and inviting her to step in, to try him and to linger. "Mr Darcy," she whispered, "I am too often impertinent. It is ill advised of you to encourage that habit in me."

"Yet, such is precisely my intent. I live in constant anticipation of what you will do or say next. What would you say, for example, if I asked to kiss you?"

"Nothing at all, for I suspect my lips would soon be more agreeably engaged."

He stood, still and expectant, watching her and saying nothing.

She arched a brow. "So, are you asking?"

"I was trying to decide if I dared."

"If you dared? Come, Mr Darcy, when have you ever failed to dare?"

"Frequently. But not this time." He set his hand boldly at her waist and pulled her close. "May I?"

She never said yes. She never even nodded. All she could later recall was wrapping her arms round his neck, claiming him as her own. His hat was a tragic casualty of the moment, but his hair was rich between her fingers, his breath as familiar as her own, and his body the safe stronghold to which she would forever cleave in times of joy or heartache.

She pressed her lips against his chin, pushing herself away by a mere inch—enough to catch her breath. "Wait... I cannot."

He stiffened, and for the first time in all their acquaintance, a look of uncertainty clouded his eye. "Elizabeth? What is it?"

She pulled the glove from her left hand and, with a hint of mischief in her expression, held up the plain gold band she yet wore. "I am still in mourning."

He snatched her hand and slipped the offending jewellery from her finger, tossing it carelessly into the trees. "There. A decided improvement."

"Mr Darcy! What sort of gentleman would discard a lady's last token of her beloved husband?" she cried in mock outrage.

"Elizabeth—" He leaned close to her ear and whispered. "In my haste, I never asked, and I never gave you a chance to tell, but upon your marriage, you were still underage. If anyone had thought to challenge it, you were never lawfully married."

She stared at her naked finger in startled dismay, then a smile grew into a shaking laugh. "What will Mama say?" she wondered aloud.

"I am more curious what she will say when you tell her you are engaged."

"I am?" She set a fist on her hip and tilted her head. "To whom do you mean to marry me this time?"

"Why, myself, of course!"

"No, no, Mr Darcy, I must protest on this occasion. A proper engagement must be accompanied by a most thorough proposal and a kiss so scandalous that the prospective bride would be too ashamed to refuse."

"That kiss was not scandalous enough? And what do you mean, 'a most thorough proposal'? Are not the words, 'Will you marry me?' sufficient to the task?"

She considered. "They might be, if I had ever heard them."

He growled beneath his breath and pulled her to himself for a kiss that left her dizzy, panting, and instinctively clinging to his neck, for her foot had somehow twined itself round his leg. "Marry me, Elizabeth."

She huffed for breath and righted her bonnet. "I certainly cannot refuse now."

He kissed her more softly this time, brushing her lips tenderly and stroking a wayward curl back from her face. "Then, my love, you will wish to inform your mother at once. I assume she will ask me to stay to tea, then I must send word to my solicitor right away to draw up the papers. Shall we shock the world and marry next month, or wait until your 'mourning' is officially complete?"

"Oh! I have no special fondness for long engagements. By all means, let us be practical, as you always are."

He wrapped an arm around her and rested his cheek on her forehead. "No hope of that. Any thought I had for my own way is long gone. From this day forward, your pleasure is all my desire."

She leaned into him. "That, I can accept."

K EEP READING MORE OF Darcy and Elizabeth's romance! Pick up your copy of
The Courtship of Edward Gardiner, and find out what happens when Darcy
and Elizabeth meet as children! Will they share an instant connection? And will Lizzy's
beloved Uncle Gardiner win the lady of his heart? Keep reading for a sneak preview of a
very young Elizabeth Bennet dressing down the handsome young Master Darcy.

From Alix

T HANK YOU FOR INDULGING with me and spending a little time with Darcy and Elizabeth.

I hope you've had a delightful escape to Pemberley. I'd love it if you would share this family with your friends so they can experience a love to last for the ages. As with all my books, I have enabled lending to make it easier to share. If you leave a review for *The Rogue's Widow* on Amazon, Goodreads, Book Bub or your own blog, I would love to read it! Email me the link at **Author@AlixJames.com**

K EEP READING MORE OF Darcy and Elizabeth's romance! Pick up your copy of *The Courtship of Edward Gardiner,* and find out what happens when Darcy and Elizabeth meet as children! Will they share an instant connection? And will Lizzy's beloved Uncle Gardiner win the lady of his heart? Check out the sneak preview on the next page!

A ND IF YOU'RE HUNGRY for more, including a free ebook of satisfying short tales, stay up to date on upcoming releases and sales by joining my newsletter:
https://dashboard.mailerlite.com/forms/249660/73866370936211000/share

www.ingramcontent.com/pod-product-compliance
Lightning Source LLC
Chambersburg PA
CBHW051944170626
46808CB00007B/2476